His Unexpected Lover

Elizabeth Lennox

CONTENTS

Chapter 1   1

Chapter 2   15

Chapter 3   32

Chapter 4   46

Chapter 5   55

Chapter 6   59

Chapter 7   64

Chapter 8   72

Epilogue   85

Excerpt from His Secretive Lover   88

Comments from the Author   92

Books by Elizabeth Lennox   93

Chapter 1

"I can't do this," she whispered to herself. "I thought I could, but it's simply too painful."

Kiera's shoulders slumped and she tried to find the answers within the depths of her martini. Unfortunately, the liquid only mocked her, small circles forming on the top and quickly dissipating as if to say, "You never should have come here."

Or maybe the glass was only telling her that a heavy-footed person was walking by.

She held her head up with her forehead, trying to figure out what to do. She'd only been at her new job for a less than a week and already she loved it. The people were fun, hard-working, extremely smart…that all added up to an ideal workplace where she was challenged to excel and stand out, but what was even better, she respected her peers. Instinctively, she knew that The Thorpe Group encouraged competition but, unlike other law firms, didn't condone the backstabbing and win-or-get-out pressure on cases. Oh, they won cases! Clients came to The Thorpe Group for legal advice from all over the country, all over the world even, because they knew that The Thorpe Group would deliver. The difference was that their success was due to a brilliant legal team versus barely ethical legal tactics.

There were other law firms out there with a similar reputation, although none as glamorous as The Thorpe Group. Gaining a few years at this firm on her resume would set her up perfectly for success wherever she wanted to go as a next step.

No, the work and the workers weren't the problem.

Even the location was great. Chicago was a fabulous city with excellent museums, a thriving art community, tons of shopping and a wide range of people with which to interact.

Nope, all of her issues were personal. She'd foolishly convinced herself that she would be able to deal with this problem but, after only a few days, she knew that the issue was bigger than she could handle.

Axel Thorpe.

She'd seen the gorgeous, huge male in the hallway earlier today. And that one sighting, just the short glimpse of the man as he walked into a conference room, was why she was here, trying to drown her problems in a martini.

Unfortunately, she realized after ordering the potent cocktail that she didn't like martinis.

She also didn't like her body's reaction to seeing Axel Thorpe again. She'd almost embarrassed herself when she'd seen him. Thankfully, she didn't think he'd seen her trip. Nor had any of her co-workers, which was at least something. She'd had to catch herself by grabbing onto a chair, which probably looked ridiculous, but mercifully, she hadn't fallen on the floor. She might have passed off the accident as just a fluke, but she'd almost fallen over the conference room table. Not something most people trip over because of its size and obvious placement in the room. But then again, most people hadn't just seen the love of their life after so many years.

Kiera sighed and took another sip of her martini. Maybe she just needed to plow through the drink. Keep forcing it down. Hopefully, the alcohol would keep her mind from replaying the scene. She would eventually feel nothing. Maybe that was the way she should handle Axel too. Just keep running into him until her body was numb from the reaction.

Perhaps today's sighting and the humiliating aftermath was just a fluke. Maybe if she just went up and spoke to him, greeted him and asked him how his day was going, she wouldn't be so flustered when she accidentally saw him. Sort of like taking an allergy shot every week to build up one's immune system.

She sighed and took another sip of her martini, her face squinching up ridiculously as she tried to swallow the foul stuff. And she had to acknowledge the stupidity of her idea. Being around him six years ago hadn't diminished his appeal or the impact he'd had on her when she was in college. Every time she'd seen him, she'd been floored. Just like today. Her knees went weak, she had trouble breathing, her whole body started shaking and she was unable to speak coherently.

Maybe it was just an allergy!

She almost giggled to herself and looked down at her drink. Was she reaching the giggle stage after only a few sips of the martini?

She pulled a file folder out of her leather bag, intending to get some work done. She wouldn't think about Axel. She would simply push him from her mind every time he entered. And if she saw him in the hallways at work? Well, she'd known that would happen when she'd accepted the position at The Thorpe Group. The man was one of the co-owners, for goodness sake. She would have been a fool to think she'd never see him.

But after so many years, she'd hoped that she was over him.

She shook her head with derision. Did one ever get over someone like Axel? He really was one in a million. She remembered the first time she'd seen him, laughing in a bar just like this one. She'd been a sophomore at Georgetown University in Washington, D.C. and he'd been clerking for a Supreme Court justice.

He'd been magnificent, she thought with a smile. So tall, so handsome and one could just see the charm and charisma oozing from the man's smile...

Six Years Earlier....

"This place is too crowded," Kiera pointed out, peering through the windows of the upscale bar in Georgetown. "Why don't we go back to our usual hangout?"

Debbie just grabbed Kiera's hand and pulled her deeper into the crowd, obviously eager to be here for some reason. "Because Brian will be there," Debbie replied, referring to her ex-boyfriend, almost yelling over the noise of the bar. "And I really don't want to run into him again. He's still angry about our breakup last week."

She quickly shifted out of the way of someone who almost spilled beer on her. "This place is a bit rowdier than the places we usually hang out," Kiera cautioned.

Debbie looked around and smiled. "It's nice! I like trying out new places and meeting new people."

Except that Debbie had invited all of their old friends here so they probably wouldn't meet anyone they didn't already know. "I'm not sure I'm feeling all that adventurous tonight, Debbie," Kiera cautioned. It wasn't so much that she wasn't into trying new things, but she preferred less crowded conditions. This bar was wall to wall people.

"Just pretend for one night," Debbie laughed back, pulling Kiera up to the bar and ordered two beers.

Kiera shook her head, but followed her friend, not sure this was such a good idea. "Fine," she agreed and tried to hide the weird feeling that had come over her suddenly. Midterms had just finished, and she had a bit of breathing room before her next paper was due, so it wouldn't be a bad thing to relax for a few hours. "We're not staying late."

Was she being too cautious? Probably, she told herself as she slipped between a couple that was heavy into a debate on the latest political wranglings. It was hard to avoid those kinds of discussions in a Georgetown bar. Not only were they mere miles from the heart of the federal buildings where real estate was so expensive, the area was teeming with history. The streets were mostly cobblestones from the colonial period and even a small townhouse would cost well over one million dollars. The cobblestones were ballast from the rum trade, but the political debates were due to the proximity of the federal government. She suspected that many of the people here were either international studies students, political science majors, or were interning for a senator or representative.

"This is awesome," Debbie called back to her, grinning from ear to ear, obviously excited to be in a new setting instead of their normal haunts. The bar was darker, probably proud of the bare bricks and heavy, wooden beams overhead that might or might not date back to the colonial period. If they weren't, Kiera doubted the owner would 'fess up to having new beams. Many of the establishments promoted the "old time" feel of their buildings by refurbishing so that the décor was reminiscent of colonial times, but with all the bells and whistles of modern conveniences. Of course, there was the one trendy bar she knew of that bragged about having bullet holes in the walls. Not that they claimed the bullets were colonial, but every bar had to have its quirks, she supposed.

She took the beer Debbie handed her and then turned around, trying to find a place to sit down. The odds of finding a chair or stool in a place this crowded would be pretty slim, she thought while her eyes surveyed the room.

Kiera noticed him the moment Debbie's back was turned. He was in a group of four or five other men, all of them laughing about something. But not him. He was staring right back at her. His eyes seemed to capture hers. That look was so powerful, his gaze so strong that it jolted her all the way down to her toes. More than just her eyes were captured. Her whole body was frozen in place, the noise and crowds, the damp smell of beer and other drinks…all of it just disappeared from her consciousness as she stared right back at him. She couldn't breathe and she couldn't pull her eyes away. She couldn't even move.

She hadn't even realized that Debbie had turned around and was trying engage her in conversation until Debbie breathed, "Who is that?"

Kiera struggled, but she was finally able to pull her eyes away and glanced at her friend. To her horror, Debbie was staring at the man! Her man! And there was a great deal of interest on Debbie's lovely features. Jealousy, hot and powerful stabbed through Kiera's body. She didn't like her friend even looking at a man she already considered to be hers.

Okay, so that was ridiculous. She couldn't claim ownership of a human being simply because they were looking at each other from across the room. But there was no way to suppress the furious feelings that surged through Kiera as her friend surveyed the tall, handsome stranger. Kiera tried to be rational about this. She had no claim on the man. But regardless, she was suddenly incensed that Debbie had dared to look at the guy. It was a sudden and all-consuming jealousy, something Kiera had never experienced before, so she wasn't sure how to handle that level of intensity. Men had never affected her in the past. To her, they were simply other human beings she could study with or joke with during non-study hours.

It was completely different with this man. And completely irrational.

Instead of revealing her jealousy, Kiera took a sip of her beer and pulled Debbie through the crowd until they couldn't see the man anymore, although Debbie's blond head kept craning at different angles to try and take another gander at him.

Debbie wasn't shy about letting a guy know she was interested. But didn't she need a bit of time to get over Brian? Debbie had just broken up with her boyfriend earlier this week! What was she doing ogling another man so quickly? It was ridiculous and disrespectful of Brian's feelings not to mention the three years they'd been together.

Kiera tried hard to ignore her jealousy, pushing Debbie to talk about classes and their friends in an effort to distract her from the gorgeous man. When a couple more friends showed up, Kiera was relieved to finally have support distracting Debbie from the man Kiera had already claimed, at least mentally. Not that she would do anything about her gnawing desire to find out more about the tall, intensely handsome man with the piercing, ice blue eyes.

Unfortunately, Kiera wasn't like Debbie. Where Kiera was shy and introverted, Debbie was the party girl, the one that pushed Kiera to get out and have more fun. Debbie also didn't hide her interest in the opposite sex. When Debbie wanted a man, she walked right up to him and started talking to him. Kiera hadn't ever felt this way, but she knew that she wouldn't go up to that man tonight. She wasn't that brave. Besides, the look he was giving her sent some scary feelings right through her body. And he hadn't even touched her! No, she couldn't handle him, so it was better to just stay away from that kind of…whatever it was.

An hour later, Kiera desperately needed to use the ladies' room. Unfortunately, the man she'd spotted earlier had been positioned right next to the hallway where the bathrooms were located. She wiggled in her chair, determined to ignore the need. But when Debbie popped up with the same intention, Kiera wasn't going to allow her to go alone. "I'll come with you," she said, determined to keep Debbie and the stranger from seeing each other again. Kiera knew she couldn't have the man. She wasn't glamorous or rich or any of those adjectives that would apply to the woman on that kind of man's arm. She was passably pretty with curly brown hair that tended to get out of control. She had a good enough figure but she wasn't any lingerie model.

In short, Kiera knew she was just an average kind of gal.

Debbie, on the other hand, was not only blond and beautiful, she had a way about her that seemed to draw men into her realm. She was fun and nice, not to mention extremely intelligent. And over the past year, they'd been good friends and study partners. But at this moment, Kiera could honestly say that she hated Debbie.

Because Kiera knew that Debbie was going to talk to the stranger. Kiera could see it in Debbie's eyes and was helpless to stop the action. Kiera felt helpless, desperate to keep Debbie from acquiring yet another conquest, but unable to come up with any ideas on how to stop her from working her magic.

Kiera had no doubt that Debbie was going to approach the man. It was in her eyes and Kiera glanced over at the man, her eyes worried as she gauged the distance between Debbie and the man.

But as soon as she found him through the crowd, she realized that he was looking at her!

Debbie was even primping, doing her best to get noticed. Kiera looked from Debbie to the stranger, wondering when he would notice the blond beauty standing next to her.

The stranger's eyes never wavered and Kiera's stomach did flip flops at the realization.

They made their way down the hallway to the ladies' room and Kiera breathed a sigh of relief. One gauntlet down, one more to go. Maybe she could get Debbie out of the bar. Maybe if they just left, Debbie wouldn't have time to set her sights on…

"Did you see him again?" Debbie gushed as they both washed their hands.

Kiera's throat constricted when she noticed the light of intent in Debbie's eyes. "I'm going to talk to him," she declared. Kiera sighed with resignation. When Debbie went on the prowl, men tended to fall to their knees and worship her.

She fluffed her blond hair one more time and Kiera wished she had done something more interesting with her out-of-control curls. They floated around her like some sort of bohemian gypsy instead of being smooth and glossy-straight like Debbie's blond hair. Debbie even had those pretty blue eyes that she could bat at any man and have him desperate to do her bidding. Kiera stared at her boring brown eyes, wishing for the first time that her face could be more interesting, more devastatingly beautiful. Her lashes might be long, but her mouth was too wide and too full, her nose too small to be anything other than cute instead of sophisticated and interesting. Her cheeks weren't gaunt, which was so hip lately. She even had a sprinkling of freckles over the bridge of her nose and her cheeks that she normally covered up with makeup but hadn't bothered tonight, much to her irritation now.

With a sigh, Kiera looked behind her at Debbie's luscious figure, wondering how long it would be before Debbie had the stranger wrapped around her pinky finger.

They stepped out of the hallway, Kiera holding her head down, not wanting to watch Debbie snag yet another man. Why couldn't her friend leave this one alone? Why couldn't she just let one, this special one, go about his business and not make him fall under her spell?

Suddenly, her path was blocked and someone was holding a beer towards her. She looked up, but all she saw was a denim clad chest. It was an extraordinarily muscular chest, she noticed. Her heartbeat picked up rapidly because she knew exactly who this man was. Her eyes continued to climb and she couldn't believe it when her light brown eyes captured the ice blue ones of her stranger.

The man was smiling down at her, not even noticing her blond friend beside her. Of course, Kiera had no idea if Debbie was still there or if she'd moved on. It was just this man, herself and her racing heart.

"I wish I could come up with some witty line to get your attention, but I'll admit, I'm stumped," he said with a deep voice that reminded her of spicy chocolate.

Kiera tried to smile. She tried to catch her breath. But with this man standing so close to her, his body heat and that incredible male scent wafting towards her, she just couldn't think. "I believe I'm in the same situation," she replied nervously.

He looked down at her hands and smiled. "I noticed you were drinking beer. I got you another one," he said, referring to the second beer he still had in his hands. "I know that was forward of me, but…"

Kiera straightened quickly, not wanting him to think she was rejecting the offer. "No, that's very kind of you," she replied, taking the beer. But her hand accidentally touched his and she felt some sort of…spark? She pulled back quickly, unsure of what was going on. Unfortunately, at the same time, he was releasing the beer. The result was both of them grabbing for the beer again, fumbling and beer spilled out, landing on her hand.

"I'm so sorry!" she gasped, horrified at how clumsy she was acting.

"My fault," his deep, sexy voice replied.

"No, really, I was the clumsy one," she countered, looking up into those blue eyes once again. And she couldn't move. Not even to take a breath. They looked into each other's eyes and it was as if the noise of the bar once again faded away leaving only the noise of her heartbeat. Time was frozen as she stood in front of this large man standing in front of her and the cold beer in her hand.

"I'm Axel Thorpe," he said softly, that deep baritone soothing over her skin like a balm.

"I'm Kiera Ward," she replied. As his large, strong hand took hers, she prayed hard that her knees wouldn't give out on her and she wouldn't throw up because she was suddenly feeling like something had just exploded inside of her stomach.

She had no idea how long they stood there like that. It could have been only a moment or it might have been a half hour. At that point in her life, she honestly could have looked into his ice blue eyes for the rest of her life.

"What are you doing here?" he asked, grabbing a napkin off of the bar and wiping down her hand.

She was struck by the strength in those hands. His denim sleeves were rolled up slightly and she could see the muscles in his forearms. She smiled, thinking the man had more than just good bones. She could tell by the controlled way he moved that there were muscles underneath that shirt to back up the height and breadth of those incredible shoulders.

She shivered and tried to pretend that she wasn't so affected by his closeness, not wanting this sophisticated man to realize how nervous she was. "I'm a student over at Georgetown."

He smiled and they discussed the various bars they'd frequented. That conversation led to their hobbies and jobs. She found out that he was one of four brothers, all of whom were in the legal profession. Kiera couldn't help but be impressed that he was clerking for a Supreme Court justice at the moment and she smiled, telling him of her goal to go to law school at Georgetown.

Kiera had no idea how long they'd talked, but one of the waitresses was wiping down tables when she finally looked around. "I think I'd better head home," she said, suddenly realizing that the bar had cleared out at some point while they were talking. She looked around for Debbie but all of her friends had left.

"I'll walk you home," Axel stated firmly and stood up himself.

She smiled up at him, relieved that their night wasn't going to end just yet. "That would be nice," she replied.

They walked through the now-quiet streets of Georgetown, the uneven brick sidewalks and centuries old townhomes adding charm and intimacy to their conversation. But too quickly, she was standing in front of the tiny townhome she shared with four other women and she silently wished that she was still living in the college dorms. Because then she'd have more time with this fascinating man since the dorms were farther away.

"Something inside of me is telling me not to kiss you," he stated as he moved closer to her. Kiera's heartbeat increased as she smiled up at him.

"But you're going to ignore that voice, aren't you?" she whispered, shocked that she could be so bold. She'd never been this way with another man before, always preferring to hold off and get to know a guy before becoming physical in any way. But there was just something about Axel that made it feel like she knew everything she needed to know about him.

"I believe I am," he replied.

She saw his eyes light up despite the darkness of the night. When his lips touched hers, Kiera pulled back, shocked by the touch. But when she saw the same reaction on his face, it warmed her, giving her a secure feeling that she wasn't alone with this strange, new feeling.

He kissed her again, his lips barely brushing hers, over and over again, just touching. Until she reached up and touched his cheek, signaling her desperate need for more. And he gave it to her. The next kiss obliterated everything she'd ever known about kissing a man. This was new, different…both terrifying and amazing. She never wanted to stop kissing this man. So when he lifted his head, she was embarrassed by how ragged her breathing was. It felt like she'd just run a marathon.

"Have breakfast with me tomorrow morning," he sort of asked and demanded at the same time.

Kiera smiled up at him. "I'd love it," she said, her fingers floating over his shoulders and arms. She wasn't sure she wanted him to kiss her again. But she was pretty sure she didn't want to stop touching him.

"I can't leave if you're going to keep doing that," he told her, his hands on her waist flexing against her skin.

Kiera's hands stopped. She bit her lip, feeling an almost physical ache at the idea of pulling her hands away.

But she did it. She took a step back and smiled up at him. "I'll see you tomorrow," she whispered, then turned and ran into the house, closing the door quietly so she didn't wake up her housemates.

She had breakfast with him the next morning, and dinner that same day. In fact, they spent almost the entire weekend together, parting on Sunday night only because he had to work and she had classes. But they also had dinner every night that week. By Friday night, when he came to pick her up at her townhouse, she jumped into his arms, wrapping her legs around his waist and kissing him with everything she had inside of her, showing him in the only way she knew how what she wanted.

Axel had caught her that evening and hadn't let her go. They drove to his apartment and Kiera didn't even see the décor until the following morning when they both realized that they hadn't taken time to eat dinner the previous night. He'd taken her into his arms in the parking lot of his apartment complex and started kissing her and they'd fallen into bed together.

He had been her first lover and he was the most tender, caring and sweet man she'd ever met.

It took her less than twenty-four hours to know that she was in love with Axel Thorpe. And every time they were together, she found him more fascinating, more amazing. They had their fights, arguments over silly things. But it was one of those relationships that was so overpowering, by the time they realized they were fighting, they were already laughing and pulling the other closer to make up and apologize.

It was all so perfect until that fateful day when he picked her up with a huge grin on his handsome face. She smiled as she slipped into his powerful, low-slung car. "What's up?" she asked, excited for whatever was making him smile. She had just finished her finals but had decided to take summer courses so she could be closer to Axel over the summer months. They'd even discussed the possibility of renting a house on the beach for the long, Labor Day weekend after her summer classes finished and the fall semester started.

He kissed her gently before starting up the engine. "I'll tell you when we get to dinner."

"Where are we going for dinner?" she asked, uncaring, as long as she could be with him. They always had stimulating conversations until he kissed her and carried her to his bed. She loved this man and couldn't believe how wonderful life was with him.

"My place," he responded. "I want you all to myself when I tell you this news."

She grinned, eager to be alone with him. They had better, livelier conversations when it was just the two of them and they didn't need to worry about interrupting people at the next table with their heated debates or the waiter arriving to interrupt them. She also loved it because she didn't have to hide her need to touch him, to kiss him. And she didn't need to hide her desire for him to take her to his bed.

She was in full agreement with his plan. "Sounds perfect to me."

It took only a few minutes to arrive at his apartment complex. And when she walked through the door of his apartment, she knew exactly what to expect. Dinner was never first on the menu. It had been the same ever since they'd met that first night in the bar. At the first touch, they were on fire for each other and Axel lifted her into his arms and carried her into his bedroom. It wasn't much to look at, just a bed and dresser. Everything about the man was utilitarian. Until he was in the bedroom. Then he was anything but.

And when it was all over, she sighed with happiness as he held her in his arms. "So what's your big exciting news?" she asked once her breathing was back to normal.

He swatted her bottom and pulled her out of bed. "Come with me," he said and pulled her out the door, refusing to let her carry the sheet with her.

Kiera grabbed his shirt just as he pulled her out the door and slipped her arms into the warm material. No matter how many times he'd encouraged her to be more casual around him, she couldn't walk around his place naked. He had no qualms though.

"Here," he said, placing several pamphlets in her hands.

She looked down at the brochures, not sure what these had to do with him. "Are you going back to school?" she asked. Her heart lurched at the possibility since these brochures were for schools in Illinois.

He pulled her closer, his hands resting lightly on her back as he kissed the top of her head. "I was hoping you might transfer to the University of Chicago."

She smiled up at him, but her smile wasn't as bright as it had been a moment ago. "Why would I do that?" she asked.

"Because I'm going back to start up the mergers and acquisitions division at The Thorpe Group, the law firm my brothers own."

She pulled back slightly. "You're leaving Washington, D.C.?" she asked, a sharp, stabbing pain shooting through her stomach and chest at the idea. "I thought you loved your job at the Supreme Court? It's such a coup to have that opportunity."

"It is, but it's also just a stepping stone. The ultimate goal all along was to figure out which type of law I wanted to practice, so I could start up and build that division in my brothers' law firm. It's a great opportunity. And when you finish school, I'm sure there would be a job there for you as well."

Kiera pulled back, appalled by the idea. "I can get my own jobs, thank you very much." She was offended that he would suggest that he get her a job somewhere. She was going to be a great lawyer! She definitely didn't need handouts!

Axel pulled her back into his arms. "Of course you can. But why would you when you could have a ready-made job waiting for you?"

She didn't like his answer one little bit. "Because I need to prove myself on my own?" she suggested sarcastically, unable to hide the hurt in her voice with his idea. Did he think she couldn't cut it on her own merits?

He laughed again, shaking his head. "I have complete faith in your abilities, Kiera. That was never a question. But if you transferred to U of Chicago, we could still be together."

She pulled back, irritated for some reason. "And what about Georgetown University?" she challenged. "It has a better reputation than the University of Chicago. I had to work very hard to get into Georgetown."

He pulled back slightly, looking down at her with eyes that were hurt at her quick rejection. "I thought you wanted to go to law school?" he asked, his shoulders straightening in the face of her resistance. It all seemed like a great plan in his mind. Why couldn't she see how perfect this was?

"I do!"

"So what's wrong with law school in Chicago?"

She couldn't believe what he was actually suggesting. "What's wrong with working in a law firm right here in Washington, D.C.? It's the center of legal activity."

He shook his head, dismissing her idea completely. "This is all politics and lobbyists. It isn't the type of law I want to practice."

Words failed her. "Are you suggesting that I give up a great school, one that I've wanted to attend since I was ten years old, just because you have a cushy job with your brother's law firm?"

Axel stood there looking down at her, confused. "I'm not sure I understand. There is no downside to this for you. Hell, Kiera, you don't even need to work if you don't want to."

Kiera stood there staring at him, not sure how to react. "I don't think I understand what you're suggesting." Her body was going numb.

Axel pulled her closer, feeling her tense muscles underneath his fingers. "I want you to marry me. I would love it if you would come back to Chicago with me and be my wife."

Her mouth fell open and her chest felt about the same but with additional pain shooting throughout her whole body. "Are you suggesting that I give up going to law school, drop out of college and just follow you so I can be your wife?"

"You don't have to give up anything. But if you wanted to, I'm just saying that's okay. You can do anything you want. I intend on making enough money to support both of us."

Kiera knew he thought this was a good deal. But to her ears, she was giving up everything and he was getting the life he always wanted. "So let me get this straight. You want me to drop out of one of the best schools in the country, follow you to Chicago so you can pursue your dream career. You're not willing to get a job here in Washington, D.C., not even look for one here that might fit your desired legal area, because you want to go back to Chicago. You want me to give up everything while you gain everything. Is that it?"

He ran a hand through his hair, frustrated with the way she was interpreting his offer. "It isn't like you have to give up everything. Just transfer schools! And we can still be together! I know you love me and I feel exactly the same for you! What's the problem here?"

"The problem is that you're not sacrificing anything and yet you're asking me to sacrifice all of my dreams!"

They stood there in his small living area, glaring at each other.

If he thought that was who she was, he didn't know her at all.

"I have to go," she whispered, hurt beyond anything by his attitude and assumptions.

"No you don't," he said, trying to calm her down. "Just stay and talk about this," he tried to coax her.

She slipped back into the bedroom and grabbed her clothes, refusing to even look at him. When she was dressed, she walked back out to his barren living room and something occurred to her. "You've never really made this into a home because you always knew you'd be going back to Chicago, right?"

He'd grabbed his jeans as well, his frustration obvious. Axel looked around his apartment, not sure what she was talking about. "What do you mean?"

"This apartment…" she said, waving her hand around to encompass the sofa and books but no television, no coffee table. There was nothing that would make one sit back and relax. "It isn't just a bachelor pad. You've never really moved in here."

"Of course I have. All of my stuff is in the closet. What would you expect me to do?"

Kiera closed her mouth, so many things falling into place. "Well, I guess I should at least be flattered that you wanted me to come with you."

He grabbed his shirt, buttoning it up partway but his frustration was obvious. "We're not finished talking about this," he said and started looking for his keys. "Let's just go out to dinner." He stopped looking for them when he noticed her chin wobbling, a sure sign that she was closer to breaking down than he thought. He sighed heavily and moved towards her, intending to take her into his arms and reassure her that they could make this work.

She pulled back when he started to touch her, not sure what she might do if she felt his hands on her back. Kiera was so hurt by his suggestion that she didn't need to work. But she was also feeling a great deal of pain caused by the fact that he wouldn't even consider finding a job here in Washington, D.C., at least until she finished school herself. He wasn't willing to sacrifice anything for her. She'd been such a fool! She'd thought he genuinely cared for her, that they had something special, but his offer explained it all to her. She was a convenience. He didn't see her as an equal partner at all, but just a good lay that he wanted to transport to his home town.

She was holding on to her emotions with all the control she had at the moment and she didn't want to break down into tears now. He already thought of her as the kind of woman who went to college to get an MRS degree, what would he think of her if she started weeping all over him, begging him to stay here with her? He'd lose even more respect for her.

She couldn't handle that. If there was nothing else, she wanted him to at least respect her.

"I'm not really hungry any more. I'll just make my own way home."

That infuriated Axel. "There's no way I'm letting you take the bus or catch a cab, Kiera. I'll drive you home. And we need to talk about this. There has to be some way to make this work."

"No!" she snapped at him, not sure if she was saying 'no' about making it work or him driving her home. "I'll get home on my own."

"Don't be ridiculous," he practically growled. "Hold on. I think my keys are in the bedroom."

As soon as he disappeared in search of his car keys, she slipped out the door. Thankfully, a cab was at the curb letting someone else off so she was able to dive into the back just as Axel was rushing out the door. Her last image of him was his furious face as the cab driver pulled away and she knew that the tears were already streaming down her cheeks.

CHAPTER 2

Current Day....

Kiera pushed the martini out of her line of sight. She wasn't going to drink it. She looked up to try and find a waitress, wanting something a bit less lethal. She was just about to raise her hand when the office manager for The Thorpe Group spotted her from another table. Kiera wanted to just slide under the table and pretend like she wasn't here, but Autumn – a stunning brunette woman – walked gracefully to Kiera's table.

"What are you doing here all alone?" she asked, smiling sincerely at Kiera. "Why don't you join us? We're about to celebrate Mia's newfound freedom, and I heard that you were instrumental in figuring out what was really going on with that sleezebag ex-fiancé of hers."

Kiera was already shaking her head when Mia Paulson herself appeared at the edge of the table. "It's you!" she gasped and bent low, hugging Kiera tightly. "I didn't have a chance to thank you for what you did earlier today! You are my hero!"

Kiera laughed, feeling painfully self-conscious, when a blond woman appeared next. Of the three new arrivals, Autumn was the tallest, but only because she was wearing three inch, spike heels that must kill her feet every day. Mia was a bit shorter, but only because her sleek black slacks and neat white shirt weren't in a style that could handle three inch heels. The latest arrival was about an inch shorter, which meant that Autumn and Mia were about Kiera's own height of five feet, six inches.

"This is our former client, Mia Paulson, but of course you already knew that," Autumn was explaining, "and this is Cricket Fairchild, who we found cursing out our beloved leader. So we kidnapped her into joining us as well, thinking she would be a perfect addition to our party." Cricket was a vivacious blond woman with startlingly intelligent eyes. She was shorter by a couple of inches, but what she lacked in height, she made up for in energy. It practically sizzled throughout her body and her blond curls bounced around her beautiful face.

The three women didn't wait for an invitation. They hustled Kiera over to their table, an empty chair already pulled over from another table. Autumn even pulled Kiera's work folder away and stuffed it back into Kiera's leather bag before turning to raise her hand, getting the attention of the waitress. "We'll have a pitcher of margaritas and four glasses please," she said with a smile to soften the request.

Kiera sat uncomfortably by the three, gorgeous women, feeling insecure and inadequate while she slowly sipped her drink. The women chatted on about Ash Thorpe and how Mia was furious with him for being so arrogant and domineering. A few "stupids" and "jerks" were thrown in there for good measure.

But as they talked, Kiera realized that, although these ladies were shockingly beautiful, they were all down to earth, funny, and more laid-back than they'd initially appeared.

"Sounds like we all have man troubles," Kiera observed, taking another sip. These women weren't intimidating. They were just like her, all in love with men who were just as irritating and obnoxious as Axel.

Of course, she wasn't in love with Axel. At least, not any more. There had been a time…

No, not going there, she told herself firmly and took another long sip of her margarita. She felt the other women's eyes on her and silently cursed herself for revealing her feelings.

"Axel?" Mia asked carefully, her eyes narrowed as she considered the woman's predicament.

Kiera was proud of herself for not cringing. "Everyone has their albatross," she replied wistfully, wishing she honestly felt nothing for Axel Thorpe.

There was a bit more chatter back and forth but Kiera suddenly stopped, feeling something strange…she wasn't sure what. She'd had too much to drink to figure it out, so she ignored the strange, oddly familiar feeling and took another long sip of her drink, still trying to get Axel out of her mind. She shook her head and set her glass down on the table. Unfortunately, the weird sensation wouldn't go away. It was almost the same feeling she'd gotten that first time…No!

"Ladies," she started to say, trying to give them a warning about…well, she wasn't sure for what. Her head was spinning and she was feeling too relaxed to feel truly threatened.

Kiera smiled wistfully as Mia admitted that she was in love with Ash. It was so sweet that she stopped thinking about Axel for a few moments and welcomed the relief.

"But he doesn't trust me," Mia was saying before sighing with frustration.

Mia almost spilled her drink when the man snuck up behind her. "Yes I do," Kiera's new boss was saying, probably in reference to trusting Mia but none of the women were completely sure. Kiera swallowed painfully, her mind still too murky to figure out the rest. But she shifted in her seat and…yep, sure enough. All four Thorpe men were standing behind them, partially hidden by the décor of Durangos, but it was obvious that they had all heard their conversation.

Her eyes lifted slowly, her heart racing in that horrible way that it always did when Axel moved around the table. And he was definitely coming nearer to their table. Or was it more grammatically correct to say closer? She wasn't sure about the appropriate grammar at the moment because her margarita-fuzzy mind was spinning with both the alcohol and his proximity.

"What are you doing here?" she whispered when he stopped right next to her. She wasn't worried. The alcohol had taken care of any nervousness for her. But there was still that zinging chemistry that was always present whenever he was around. She'd thought the years would diminish the impact of his body so close to hers, but the truth was, the years had only made the affect more acute. She should have realized that when she'd almost tripped earlier today after just a glimpse of him in the hallway.

Axel looked down at the obviously inebriated but still shockingly beautiful woman that had haunted him for years. Damn, he'd missed looking at those freckles. She looked so sophisticated and untouchable with her lush curls flying everywhere and her brown eyes drawing him closer, as if she could read his soul.

She was a bit thinner now than she'd been in college. Definitely more sophisticated with her power suits and her killer heels. But he knew what was underneath those suits and it drove him nuts that he couldn't strip away all those layers and get to the real woman underneath. He wanted to see the woman who writhed in his arms or laughed at his jokes, challenged his arguments.

He wasn't sure if he was angry with her or thrilled that she was finally here in Chicago. "I'm going to drive you home," he explained, picking up her leather bag and her purse and tucking both under his arm as he took her hand and pulled her out of her chair.

"I don't want to go home," she shot back, her voice breathy and nervous. She stumbled slightly, not sure if that was because she'd had too much to drink or because her legs were always wobbly whenever she was close to Axel, but his arm immediately wrapped around her waist, pulling her hard against his muscular body. "Don't hold me like that," she commanded, but even that order was said without much force.

He turned slightly so he was holding her against his chest, enjoying the view of her cleavage from this angle. He took in her unfocused gaze and the soft curls that had escaped the clasp at the back of her neck. She looked so soft and sexy, and she had no idea how gorgeous she was. Men stopped and stared at her and she was oblivious. From a distance, she looked like some sort of sexual siren, luring men closer but once they saw her, many pulled back, struck by how lovely she was. Those adorable freckles only confused the issue. Years ago, he'd been thrilled to know that he was the only man who knew that the freckles were only on her face.

He hated the idea that another man, possibly more than one, had held her incredible body, experienced her passion, and discovered that the rest of her lush body was covered in milk white skin without a blemish anywhere.

Right now, her hands were resting against his chest and he didn't say a word. There was a point when he'd thought he'd never have her soft, gentle hands on him again but here she was, holding onto him like a lifeline. "Are you going to fall over?" he asked, looking down into her expressive brown eyes with amusement, enjoying her dependence on him, even if it only lasted until she sobered up.

Kiera narrowed her eyes and her adorable tongue poked out of her mouth, as if she were trying to evaluate the possibility of falling over. "I haven't decided," she told him honestly, then berated herself for that honesty. "But I don't need your arm around me either way." Unfortunately, she didn't have the will or the ability to move out of his arms. He was stronger than she was by a significant margin, but there was also his warmth seeping into her body that she'd desperately missed since she'd walked out of his apartment all those years ago. Standing here with his arms around her, she realized that she hadn't been warm since the last time he'd held her. And that warmth had absolutely nothing to do with the air temperature and everything to do with how he made her feel inside.

He didn't let go of her but, instead, turned her around so they were walking out of the bar. "Let's get you some coffee," he said.

"I don't want coffee either," she grumbled. She wanted to stand there in his arms, revel in just being close to him and how wonderful it felt. But there wasn't much to do about it since he was walking her out the door. Thankfully, she wasn't so far gone that she said anything to him about how much she liked his arms around her. Yes, at least she'd held that back, not wanting to make a fool of herself.

"Tough," Axel replied, chuckling to himself because this was the first time he'd ever seen Kiera drunk. He liked it actually. He was enjoying the soft feel of her body against his, her gentle curves that he remembered so vividly. This woman had appeared in his dreams over the years so often, he'd actually cursed her when he'd woken up. "You probably need some food too, don't you?"

"Not at all," she countered, proud that she could say that she wasn't the least bit hungry.

"What have you eaten tonight?" he asked, evaluating how far gone she really was. She was leaning against him but she wasn't stumbling. That was a good sign.

Damn he'd missed her! He hadn't let himself admit it all these years, but having her here, in his arms tonight, he knew that a part of him had never felt alive after she'd walked out of his life. And he'd let her! That was the worst part.

But now she was here. He'd known that Ash was hiring her. The four brothers discussed all hiring decisions before they were finalized, except for the support people who Autumn managed. But when Kiera's name had come up, her brothers had instantly been impressed, eager even to bring her on board. She had outstanding credentials and had more trial expertise under her belt than all the other candidates, several of whom were older than she was. What could he have told his brothers? No, you can't hire the best trial lawyer to come out of law school in the past five years because I might just toss her in bed and never let her out again? Axel didn't think that would go over too well with his brothers.

Unfortunately, when he'd seen her earlier this afternoon, even after he'd known to be expecting her in the hallways, he'd still felt like someone had punched him in the gut. Over the years, she'd grown even more beautiful than she'd been while in college. Back then, she'd had a sort of innocent-bohemian quality to her. She'd been casual and laid back but in an oddly intense sort of way.

Now she was all polished and sexy – with those professional suits that he wanted to just peel away and find out what she wore underneath.

He tucked her into his car, almost groaning as she crossed her legs with those damnable heels that made her legs look even sexier. He stared at her legs, unaware of what he was doing until he heard a noise behind him. He'd just drive her home, make sure she was safe and then head home himself.

"Where do you live?" he asked when he slipped into the leather seat beside her.

When he got no response, he looked over at her and was surprised to find that she'd fallen asleep.

"Well, hell," he thought with a chuckle. "I guess I'll just have to drive you to my place," he told the sleeping beauty. The idea didn't bother him one little bit. In fact, he preferred it this way.

He drove through the night, his body on fire for the woman in the passenger seat but, more importantly, he was more relaxed now than he had been in…years. He had his Kiera right where he wanted her.

Well, not exactly, he thought. He might put her in his bed to let her sleep off the tequila, but unfortunately, he couldn't share that bed with her.

As he carried her into his house, he thought about the conversation the four women had been having before he and his brothers interrupted. Kiera had said, "We all have man troubles." But did that mean that she was as attracted to him as Autumn was to Xander? Or did that mean she had another man she was interested in? Was she seeing someone? She'd only been in town for a few days, having moved here from San Francisco, where she'd taken a job right out of college. She'd graduated from Georgetown Law School with honors and had been a hot commodity, he knew. He'd watched her career, followed her through his acquaintances and knew that she'd excelled at criminal law.

He thought back again to the conversation at the bar earlier tonight and smiled at the thought of the cute woman who had just gotten free of a murder charge. She was sweet in a fluffy kind of way. He was pretty sure that Ash's problems were over tonight. The four of them had been discussing Ash's upcoming nuptials in Ryker's office before they'd found out that all four women had gone to Durango's to celebrate Mia's freedom.

Axel laid the still sleeping Kiera on his bed and contemplated Ash's reaction tonight about the conversation between the women. Ash was going to propose to Mia, Axel thought. Well, maybe he'll wait until the morning. Axel wasn't sure that Mia would understand anything Ash asked her tonight.

Axel considered his woman, laying curled up on his bed, exactly as he'd pictured her so many times over the years. Well, not quite exactly as he'd imagined her. She'd been naked in his dreams.

He bent down and took off her shoes, smiling slightly when her toes curled up as if they'd been scrunched into the shoes for too long and were now aching to be free of all restrictions. He held the shoe in his hand, looking from the shoe to her foot with fascination. In college, she'd worn sneakers or flats and he'd been turned on every time she'd come near him. Now he had to contend with these sexy heels that made her legs look several feet longer? He was a gonner!

He smiled, enjoying the possibility of getting lost in Kiera's newest form of sexy. He wouldn't mind having that kind of trouble one little bit.

She needed to be comfortable, he thought as he took in her dark lashes against her pale, white skin. And as a gentleman, wasn't it his duty to help her sleep off the alcohol in comfort? Besides, this dress had probably cost her couple hundred dollars at least. She would ruin it if she slept in it. And Axel really didn't want her to blame him if she ruined her dress. It would get all wrinkled because he knew that she snuggled up in her sleep in a way that would bunch the tailored material up around her waist.

It was such a lovely dress too!

His fingers moved carefully down her back, letting the zipper slide through the material, itching to touch the skin slowly revealed to his hungry eyes. But he kept his fingers on the fabric and not on her soft, silken skin. He peeled the dress down over her shoulders and legs, almost groaning when she shifted her body to make the process easier. He almost suspected she was awake and tormenting him, but then she sighed in her sleep. He knew from past experience how she slept. He'd stayed awake several nights just watching her, enjoying the way she curled up next to him. He remembered how her warm breasts pressed against his chest. He remembered many nights when he'd felt those breasts, felt the way she'd rubbed against him in her sleep. It didn't matter if they'd just made love throughout the night, every time she'd done that, he'd wanted to roll her over and make love to her again. In his mind, her breasts had been absolutely perfect and he'd never gotten tired of exploring their sensitive, pink peaks or the soft, white mounds.

Well, to be honest, he'd thought everything about her was perfect. He'd enjoyed hours in bed with her, exploring every part of her body. She'd protested at times, even fighting him back in an effort to get the upper hand sexually but even back then he'd been stronger and he'd always won their tussles. He'd pin her to the bed and have his way with her, taking his time tasting, kissing and enjoying every inch of her delicate skin despite her screams of frustration and need. It had only turned him on more when she'd done that.

Damn! His body was hard and aching for her and he hadn't even touched her. No woman had ever had this kind of power over his body. Not before he met her and certainly not after.

He carefully hung the dress up in his closet, enjoying the sight of her dress mixed in with his suits and tailored shirts before moving back to the bed, pulling the soft blanket from the bottom of the bed up to cover her. He refused to let his eyes wander over that pretty black bra. Nor would he allow his eyes to explore that black, lace thong! Why the hell was she wearing a thong?

Hell, now he was going to picture her every day, in every one of her professional suits wearing some color of thong!

This was not fair!

He almost slammed his bedroom door as he stormed out of the room. After a pointless cold shower, he flopped onto the bed in one of his spare bedrooms. He'd always loved this house with the extra bedrooms and lots of space. He lived further out of the city than his brothers, but that allowed him much more privacy. He had ten acres of land and his house sat right in the middle of it. He had a couple of horses that he enjoyed riding and even a vegetable garden that he tended on the weekends. Unlike Ash who enjoyed working with wood and Xander who worked out at the gym like a fiend, he'd found gardening to be a great stress reliever. He had no idea what Ryker did to relieve the stress of work related issues. He wasn't even sure if Ryker acknowledged stress. In fact, now that he thought about it, he suspected that his oldest brother worked to relieve the stress of work. All four of them regularly showed up at the gym for sparring in the boxing ring so perhaps that was what Ryker did to let off steam.

He stared up at the ceiling, wondering what Kiera did for relaxation now. Did she live in one of the apartments closer in to the city? Or did she prefer being in the outer suburbs, wanting more fresh air and space?

The distance from the city tended to be a hassle sometimes. The traffic could be bad, but since he worked long hours, most of his drives into or back from work were during off hours, often early in the morning before most people were coming into the city for work or later in the evening when they were already at home and eating dinner. When he had to stay in the city late at night for a social event or because of work, he would simply crash at one of his brothers' places for the night. They reciprocated by coming out to his place on the weekends to ride his horses or just hang out and eat his fresh produce.

Thinking of Kiera in the other room made him smile with satisfaction. He'd wanted her here for so long. All the years, all the changes to this house, he knew now that he'd always had her preferences in the back of his mind. He wasn't sure about all of them, and he hadn't even been aware of doing it, but he'd built this house with her in mind based solely off of the conversations they'd had during their short time together six years ago.

He'd worked hard to renovate this old house and the barn behind it. He'd done some of the work himself but Ash had helped him with a lot of the more complicated issues of restoring an old house. Ash was much better at woodwork but between the four of them, they'd gotten this place in shape and he loved it. It might still look old, but there were modern conveniences all over.

In fact, it reminded him of that bar where he'd first seen Kiera. The late evening sunshine had been lighting her hair on fire. In normal light, she looked like a gorgeous brunette. But that day, with the sun behind her, the light had sparked diamonds all through her curls, turning some of them to red and auburn mixed in with the darker colors. He'd been fascinated by her hair even before he'd looked into her soft, chocolate eyes.

Rolling over, he punched his pillow, forcing thoughts of his former lover out of his mind. Or at least trying. He couldn't completely obliterate her from his thoughts because she was only one wall away from him. He didn't get much sleep that night, thinking about Kiera back in his bed after all these years. So when the sun woke him up, he gave up on trying to get back to sleep. He checked on Kiera and found her to be still sleeping. He quietly grabbed a pair of jeans, showered and went downstairs to his favorite place in the house. The kitchen.

The kitchen was a large, brick and stone room with a huge stove off to one side, a double oven and even an inside grill for those days when it was too cold to get outside and grill steaks, chicken or whatever he wanted. There were lots of windows and light coming in with roughhewn rafters and a cabin feel to the room. It was huge and spacious and designed around how he liked to cook. All of his brothers enjoyed cooking, but none of his brothers had his gardening talents. Not that they would know it since they all lived in the city with no place to even try their hand at gardening. Which meant that they were constantly nagging him for tomatoes, cucumbers and whatever else he'd planted in the spring.

This year, he was having a bumper crop of peppers. There were banana peppers, green, red and yellow peppers and, his favorite, jalapeno peppers. Grabbing a bowl, he walked outside barefoot and snagged a fresh, red tomato off the vine, some jalapenos and banana peppers and then bent down to dig out an onion and a potato from his potato barrel. He felt like a Spanish omelet, he thought as he came back inside and started coffee.

He smiled at the thought of Kiera waking up. He wished he could be there to watch it but he stayed downstairs, making coffee and reading the newspaper while he waited for her to stir.

When he finally heard her move upstairs, he poured a cup of coffee for her, adding in a touch of sugar, then brought it up the stairs.

"Good morning," he said, leaning against the doorway as he watched her look around, trying to get her bearings.

Kiera pushed her out-of-control hair back from her eyes and looked around, not recognizing anything but the man standing in the doorway. She blamed her dry mouth on the drink last night and not on the fact that the man wasn't wearing a shirt and those jeans hung low on his slim hips. Her reaction had absolutely nothing to do with those muscles rippling along his lower abdomen, or the amazingly ripped shoulders and biceps the man had developed.

This definitely wasn't fair, she thought with increasing resentment as she tried to hold the soft blanket in front of her. "Where am I?" she asked, her voice hoarse. She was already embarrassed that she was wearing only her favorite black, lace underwear but now she was self-conscious that she was so affected by the man standing in the doorway looking like some sort of Greek god and she had no idea where she was or what happened last night after getting into his car. The leather seats had been so comfortable and she'd been so tired. It had been a long, first week at her new job, punctuated at the end with the traumatic sight of the man she…not loved anymore, but of the man she'd loved at one time in her life. A time long ago.

"At my house," Axel replied, moving into the room and handing her the cup of steaming hot coffee. "You look like hell," he commented.

Kiera didn't bother to argue with him. She knew she looked awful but her highest priority right at the moment was caffeine. He could say just about anything right now but until she had coffee, she wasn't going to argue with him.

She sat back against the pillows, feeling painfully self-conscious as she gripped her coffee in both hands while desperately trying to hold onto the blanket as well. She honestly wasn't sure which was the more important task, getting caffeine into her system or hiding her body from his too-knowing eyes. "Why am I at your house?" she asked.

One sardonic eyebrow went up and he smiled slightly. "Because you were too drunk last night to tell me where you lived."

Her eyebrows went up with that bland statement. "You didn't bother to read my driver's license?" she asked with rising anger.

He tilted his head. "Hm…I didn't think of that," he replied. He hadn't thought about it because he'd wanted her here. Case closed.

She bit her lip and looked around, her fingers trying to bring the blanket higher but that uncovered her toes. She curled her legs underneath her, not wanting any additional skin to show. She remembered too vividly what he liked to do when he saw skin and mentally she wasn't able to fight him off. Not that he would try anything, she told herself. They'd finished together long ago. There was no reason he might want her now. "Did we…?" she asked, leaving the statement hanging.

He knew exactly what she was asking and decided to have a bit of fun with her. "Did we make love?" he asked, and enjoyed the fire that sparked into her eyes. "Did you scream out with your release the way you used to whenever I touched you?" He waited for his words to sink in. "Did we spend the whole night in each other's arms, satisfying the craving that obviously hasn't died out even after years of being apart?"

"Stop it," she whispered, her tongue darting out and licking her lips, feeling the need start to throb once again inside of her. She didn't want to feel this way about Axel. He'd broken her heart once and it had taken her a long time to start living again. She might have walked out on him that night, but he'd pushed her out the door with his assumptions that she'd drop everything to follow him when he wouldn't sacrifice anything for her. She'd been devastated that semester, not even able to take summer classes because she'd been so upset about his betrayal.

"Stop what?" he asked, his eyes looking down at hers with that heat, that intensity she'd never been able to ignore. "Stop saying what we both want?" he suggested. He didn't move into the room, staying right there in the doorway but it didn't matter. His presence was more powerful than movement or space. "Or stop offering what you so desperately need?"

"Just stop talking," she said and slid her legs to the left, getting up off the bed. It was difficult since she wouldn't relinquish either the blanket or the coffee cup.

Axel watched her, shaking his head. "You never were able to walk around naked with me, were you?" he teased.

Her head snapped around and she blushed. "Where are my clothes?" she demanded, trying for dignity but knowing that she was losing that battle. Especially when he was watching her so closely, those ice blue eyes never leaving her body even though the blanket covered most of her skin.

"In the closet," he said, leaning back and watching her, enjoying the way she walked and held herself. She was grace personified and he wished she'd just give in and accept that what they'd had all those years ago hadn't died out from lack of communication. If anything, his need for her was stronger. He couldn't believe how intensely he wanted to grab her and make love to her, to touch every part of her delectable body.

He pushed away from the door and turned around, trying to shift slightly to accommodate his reaction to her in his bedroom once again. "I hope you're hungry," he called out as he made his way down the hallway. "I'm making Spanish omelets." He wasn't giving her mercy from his watchful gaze so much as he was giving himself a bit of mercy by moving away from her. A man could only take so much enticement, he told himself.

Kiera watched as he walked out, wishing she could tear her eyes away and remain immune to his physique. But then, what woman wouldn't watch? The man was a god!

When he was gone, she sighed and clasped the blanket around her more securely and took another fortifying sip of coffee.

"Spanish omelets?" she repeated suddenly.

Her stomach growled and she realized that she hadn't eaten anything since she'd had some yogurt yesterday morning for breakfast. She'd seen Axel just before she was going to grab lunch and hadn't had the stomach for anything after that. And then she'd been drinking with the ladies last night and…she thought carefully…nope, no food for dinner either. There had been chips and salsa, but Kiera knew she'd been too busy trying to drown out the memory of Axel's presence on her mind and body to worry about anything nutritious.

She opened several doors, finding a bathroom that was made of white and grey wood. Very rustic, she thought with envy. There were skylights overhead and the shower was more like a large room enclosed with glass but with big, smooth stones as the outer walls and matching tiles on the floor. She blushed, thinking of Axel in that space, the hot water rushing over those muscles and…

She shook her head and looked around. After freshening up, she finally found the closet that had been hiding her dress and pulled it back on. But she didn't put her shoes on, carrying them downstairs instead. She felt a bit silly walking barefoot through Axel's domain. But she couldn't deny that she was fascinated by all that she was seeing. His large, spacious house was a far cry from the undecorated apartment he'd lived in before. This house even had plants! She loved indoor plants, thinking they gave an area a sense of vibrancy and health. She'd always had plants in her living areas until she'd moved to San Francisco. At that point, she knew she wasn't going to be living there forever so she hadn't wanted to have plants that might not get the attention they needed with her long hours of work.

After searching through the other rooms and not feeling guilty in the slightest, she found Axel in the kitchen and almost swooned with the space and light not to mention the ultra-sleek kitchen equipment. She stared at the convection ovens and the shiny stove with six burners and all the newest gadgets that made cooking so much fun.

And then there was Axel cooking. Still without a darn shirt and looking so delicious that her mouth almost fell open. She should have been prepared for that. He'd shown up in the bedroom doorway without a shirt, why would he stop and put one on now? It was Saturday, he was obviously relaxed in his home and wanting to be comfortable. It didn't matter that his bare chest was making her very, very uncomfortable.

Looking around, she was stunned by how homey and yet still spacious this kitchen felt. The stone and brick should normally be one or the other, but the two seemed to mesh together perfectly, reminding one that this was an older home, a place that had protected generations of families over the years. The hardwood floors were probably original to the house, but had been sanded and stained to a glossy finish, adding warmth to the whole atmosphere.

She turned and faced the man, a thought occurring to her. "Are you married?" she asked, furious and hurt, feeling horribly betrayed. Deep down inside, she knew she had no right to feel that way, but she waited tensely for him to answer her question, ignoring the painful hurt at the possibility.

Axel stood at the stove, the omelet finished but frozen in mid-air. "Married?" he asked, noting the fury in her beautiful eyes. "Why do you think I'm married?" he asked, slicing the omelet in half and sliding it expertly onto two plates.

The idea of Axel being married hurt more than she could handle. And the way he hadn't answered immediately terrified her right down to her soul. "Answer the question!" she demanded, storming over to the island, taking in more of the homey details and feeling sick suddenly. Had a woman actually been in here and made it look so warm and comfortable? Had Axel married at some point over the past six years? It wasn't an impossibility, she told herself but she desperately didn't want it to be true.

"No. I'm not married. Now tell me why you would ask me something like that."

He refilled her coffee cup, then carried the two plates over to the table that was doused in sunshine from the large windows that looked out over pastures and gardens.

She pushed the dizzying relief away to examine at another, more private, moment. "Because of all this," she said, gesturing widely at all the warmth in his kitchen with her shoes still dangling from her fingertips.

"This?" he asked, looking around. "What's wrong with this?" He'd always loved this room. He'd thought she would like it as well.

"Your house!" she came back with confusion, sure that he was lying about his marital status. "This isn't like your other place. This is..." she looked around, shaking with her anger and betrayal, "nice!" she finally finished.

Axel watched her for another moment, then burst out laughing. He set the two plates down on the table, adding a generous portion of browned, seasoned potatoes. "Well, I'm glad you like my home," he replied, then poured her some fresh squeezed orange juice. "But I'm not married."

His words instantly settled her stomach and she relaxed, almost light-headed from relief. "You did all this yourself?" she asked, her eyes wide with hope and fear.

"Sit," he told her, smothering his laughter at her disbelief. "Eat something."

Kiera looked at the omelet and her stomach growled. So instead of ignoring him or even arguing with him any longer, she took a seat at his sunny breakfast table, setting her shoes down next to her on the wide-plank floor. When she took her first bite, she closed her eyes in bliss. "This is incredible!" she gasped, forking another bite into her mouth. "Who made these?" she asked, looking for the box from the restaurant.

Since she'd watched him slide the omelet onto the plate, he rolled his eyes at her question. "I made them. Obviously," he told her, refilling her cup of coffee.

Her eyes widened. He'd cooked for her in the past, but nothing this good. It had been mostly sandwiches or a quick burger. More often they'd gone out to restaurants. Cheap ones if she were buying and more expensive ones when he could convince her to let him pay for the meal.

"When did you learn to cook?" she asked, taking another bite of the fluffy, cheesy, vegetable filled omelet. "This is incredible!" she exclaimed.

"Thanks," Axel said, taking a long sip of his cold orange juice. "As for when I learned to cook, I picked it up here and there. All my brothers cook so I guess I learned from them. And once I got into it, I liked looking up new recipes although most of what I cook is pretty simple."

She sighed as if she were in heaven. She couldn't remember ever tasting anything so flavorful. "Is that a jalapeno in the mixture?" she asked, not believing that he would be creative enough to think about putting a spicy vegetable into an egg mix.

"Yes. I grow them myself. Sometimes they aren't very spicy but this year was a good crop."

Her hand froze as she looked across the table at him. "You grow your own jalapenos?" she asked, stunned and somewhat disbelieving.

"And tomatoes and other vegetables. I grew all the stuff in your meal except for the eggs and the cheese," he said and winked at her. He knew exactly what she was thinking and loved that he'd surprised her. Kiera was one of those down to earth women who wasn't easily surprised so this was one for the books.

"I don't believe you," she came back and took another bite. "And even if you have a vegetable garden, you probably hire someone to do all the growing for you, don't you?"

He laughed, shaking his head at her disbelief. "Of course not. In fact, I'll take you out to my garden after breakfast." He looked down at the floor where her dressy shoes were laying next to her bare feet. "Of course, you'll have to borrow a pair of my boots."

She peered over the table as well but looked at his feet instead of hers. "I don't think they'll fit."

He shrugged his shoulders. "Suit yourself. But you're looking at my garden. I can't have you thinking I'm a liar."

She laughed, still disbelieving but impressed that he would even have a garden.

Kiera shook her head again, then turned back to her plate, starving for more food and the omelet was exactly what her body needed, lots of protein and veggies.

"Okay, let's go," he said when she was finished.

She blinked and looked up at him. "You're taking me home? I can just..."

"I'm taking you out to my garden. And then perhaps I'll drive you home. Don't you dare tell me that you're catching a cab because you'll be severely punished if you think about doing that again."

Kiera knew that both of them were thinking about the last time they'd seen each other which had been through the window of a cab as Kiera ran away from him.

Instead of answering him, he lifted a pair of boots he'd pulled out of his mudroom. "Put these on."

Kiera couldn't help it. She burst out laughing, never having seen this side of Axel before. She'd spent hours arguing with him about various legal issues, political topics, preferences on food and the best hamburgers. He was the ultimate intellectual in her mind. But at this moment in time, he actually looked eager to show her the garden he apparently was proud of working.

She looked down at the boots, not sure what to think. Taking them out of his hands, she slipped her heels off her feet and gestured to the door. "Lead the way. I'm fascinated by the mighty Axel's vegetable garden." She quickly slipped her feet into his huge boots, unconcerned about how silly she looked in them.

He raised one eyebrow at her cynical tone. "You still don't believe me, do you?" he asked as he opened the door and stepped back so she could precede him out doors.

She stepped onto the cement stoop and shrugged her shoulders. "Let's just say I'm ready to be convinced."

As soon as she looked around, she stopped in stunned amazement. "Axel, it is gorgeous out here!" she gasped, seeing all the amazing hues of bright orange and red, yellow and even a bit more green as the last gasp of summer held onto the leaves.

"Thanks," he said, picking up a water bucket that had fallen over, placing it back against the wall.

The way he was handling the bucket made her suspect something she wasn't prepared for. "Axel, did you plant all of this as well?" she asked, not sure what to believe now.

"Yes," he said simply, looking around at the bushes that were staggered along the pathway, interspersed with perennial flowers.

She stared up at him, seeing the pride on his face and knew that he wasn't teasing her. "I'm impressed," she said softly, her admiration for all that he'd achieved showing through in her eyes.

He took her on a tour not just of his vegetable garden but also of the entire back yard. There was a small pond at the corner of his property where the horses could drink from but he'd also built a small sitting area, complete with a wisteria covered pergola. "This is beautiful," she gasped as she stepped onto the stone patio, looking up at the changing leaves. "Did you build this as well?"

"Yes. With Ash's help. Xander and Ryker helped a bit but Ash is the one who designed it."

She stared up in wonder at all the details, impressed with the curly corners and the way the wisteria plant twisted over the top. She could easily imagine the wisteria flowers flowing down through the wood in the springtime, creating a lovely, purple cover draping down. "I love this!" and she smiled up at him.

"The garden is over here," he said, smiling because he'd been thinking of her reading in a big, comfortable chair underneath that wisteria. Take it slow, he told himself. They'd probably taken things too quickly the last time and he'd blown it. Now that she was here, he suddenly knew how much he wanted her to stay.

He led her through more bushes that grew up high, forming a wall where he'd set up a stone pathway. At the end of the path, there was an open area with raised beds filled with plants that looked pretty rough except for the deep red tomatoes, the dangling cucumbers that seemed to be greener than normal. In fact, all the vegetables in his garden looked to be much more vibrant and colorful than what she normally saw in the grocery store.

She stared, still not believing that he actually did all this but she could easily tell that this was not a professional garden. It wasn't messy so much as just…well used.

"Okay, I'm convinced," she laughed.

"So next time I tell you something, you're going to believe it, right?"

Kiera looked up and realized that he was closer than she'd thought. Her breath caught in her throat and she tried to take a step backwards, but the garden fence was behind her. "I think…" She felt trapped but didn't really want to remove herself from the trap. For so long, she'd remembered the strength and power of Axel's body, the way his arms would wrap around her or the way his hands would touch her, as if she were his woman and she'd never wanted any other man to touch her like that.

"I think you should come back up to the house and let me make love to you." He stared at her, his ice blue eyes demanding that she follow through with his suggestion.

She thought about it long and hard. There was no question that that intense chemistry was still there between them. Her body wouldn't mind experiencing the mind-blowing release that only Axel could give her.

But in the end, she simply couldn't risk it. She'd been so hurt the last time and she'd trusted him completely six years ago only to have him turn around and break her heart because he hadn't been willing to make any sacrifices for their relationship. He'd wanted her to do it all. In her mind, that only proved that she'd been more invested in their love than he had been. Or maybe not, because she hadn't been willing to drop everything and follow him. Or maybe he hadn't loved her enough to sacrifice. Maybe they had both been too young and stubborn.

Either way, she'd been too hurt and she couldn't go through it again.

"I need to go home," she said softly and looked away. She didn't bother to wait for him but trudged through the yard back to his house. Inside his mudroom, she took off the boots and placed them carefully to the side while she slipped her own feet inside her shoes.

"I'll call a cab," she said.

Axel was furious at the suggestion. It was just like it had been that last time, both of them angry and hurt and all she wanted to do was run away. Not this time. "I'll drive you," he snapped at her.

Slow down, he told himself. He had to be practical about this. Kiera was here, he had to show her that they could work together. He had to show her that they could build upon their past and make this time work out.

Unfortunately, he didn't want to be practical and he was having a damn hard time slowing down. He had been watching her walk through his garden, enjoying her being there but also knowing what was underneath that dress. His mind could vividly picture her body in that black lace and he wanted to strip off the clothes and show her exactly what they could be like together.

Instead, he grabbed his keys and headed out the door to his garage. He wouldn't let her even turn towards the front door and slammed the passenger seat closed once she was seated inside.

When he was sitting in the driver's seat, he took a deep breath and calmed down. "I'm sorry, Kiera. I know that was out of line. But I remember what it was like with you, how good we were be together." He turned to look at her, his blue eyes intense and unrelenting. "We will be together again, Kiera. Count on it," he said.

Without another word, he started up the car and backed out of his garage. It took barely twenty minutes to reach her apartment building and the only words spoken between the two of them were her directions. When she reached her building, she jumped out but just before she was about to slam the door and race inside, she bent down and stopped. "Thank you for your help last night. I appreciate the breakfast too. And the tour of your garden."

With that, she closed the door and walked into her building with as much dignity as possible even though she knew that he was staring at her the whole time.

CHAPTER 3

"Are you ready?" Autumn asked, popping into Kiera's office just before five o'clock.

Kiera looked up, then quickly back at her computer. "Just one more thing," she said and typed in several more words to the brief she was working on. "Okay," and she pressed the save button. "Let's go!" She grabbed her duffel bag and followed Autumn into the ladies' room. "So who else is on the team?" she asked as she dove into one of the stalls to change from her business suit to shorts and her newly minted softball shirt Autumn had given her just that morning.

"There are ten of us. You'll replace Samantha who left for her honeymoon last week. We're in first place so far, but Ash's team is not far behind us." Kiera was putting her jacket on the hook of the bathroom stall when she heard the next few words. "Axel is pretty good at keeping everyone motivated but we're all competitive."

"Axel?" Kiera squeaked out, her heart racing just at the man's name. She'd impulsively agreed to be on the law firm's softball team yesterday, simply as a way to get more involved socially with her co-workers as well as to stop thinking about Axel. She held her breath as she silently prayed that her plan hadn't just backfired on her.

"Sure. He's the captain," Autumn explained, although her voice was muffled as she pulled a shirt over her head. "But don't worry. He's a great coach and will help you through your turn up to bat."

Kiera leaned her forehead against the cool metal of the bathroom stall, closing her eyes and trying to figure out a way to get out of this game. For all of her efforts at staying away from the man, she was failing miserably. After seeing his home last weekend and knowing that he still wanted her, the man was constantly on her mind.

She'd tried to be strong, but every time she saw him in the hallway or if he happened to walk by a conference room when she was inside, her mind was devoid of focus for several minutes. And those were the good moments because she was sitting down in the conference meetings. When she passed him in the hallway, her balance was actually affected because she wanted him so badly. When was his impact on her going to dull?

She stared at her softball outfit, wishing she'd brought something else to wear. Unfortunately, she hadn't completely unpacked so she'd just reached into the box of clothes that contained her summer outfits and grabbed a pair of shorts, knowing it was going to be one of those hot, fall days. Since the shorts were all she had, she pulled them on, then the softball shirt and hat, making sure her hair was tucked up and tied back so it wouldn't get in her eyes. Taking a deep breath, she stepped out of the bathroom stall, mentally giving herself a pep talk.

She could deal with this, she told herself as she turned on the cold water and ran it over her wrists. She just had to be casual about this, show him that she could handle the two of them working together and playing together on the firm's softball team. She was a lawyer in his firm now which meant there would be other social situations in which they would need to interact with each other. She'd have to figure out a way to handle them better. So far, no one had picked up on her blank moments, or if they had, they hadn't made any connection with Axel's presence. She'd hate to think her co-workers might know about how she felt about the man.

Well, to be perfectly honest, Axel was a big topic of conversation in the kitchens so a lot of women were pretty obsessed with him. All four of the Thorpe brothers were subjects of conversations. The ladies in the office were constantly talking, speculating, eyeing their bosses whenever possible. Who wouldn't? The Thorpe brothers as a group were gorgeous and sexy, charming and brilliant. There really wasn't a better catch for a single woman. But there was a down side to all of this speculation, she knew. Xander's dating habits were legendary, apparently. There were bets going about how long his current lady love would last. The record was four weeks so word was out that Xander Thorpe was a player. A charming and very sweet player, but his reputation was cause for a betting pool to be constantly be under way.

Ash was the one brother Kiera didn't hear much about, except when she was out with Mia lately. After their drinking-fest last week, the four of them had gotten together for dinner on Sunday night. It was interesting how cute Mia was now that it was out that she was engaged to Ash Thorpe. She was even sporting a huge diamond ring that was definitely drool worthy.

Ryker Thorpe was the only one that no one speculated about in the office. Oh, the women definitely had the hots for him. Kiera didn't understand that because she thought Axel was the most handsome of the four brothers. Ryker was more intimidating than anything else. As the oldest, he also appeared to be the most stern which basically translated into terrifying. Generally, he always had a scowl on his handsome features.

"Ready?" Autumn asked, stepping out in a pair of cute shorts which made her long legs appear a mile long. "You look great!" she exclaimed.

Kiera looked at her own shorts, thinking they hadn't been this short the previous summer. She peered at her bottom as inconspicuously as possible and cringed. Nope, these definitely had not been this short last year. They covered her bottom but only about an inch below that.

"Come on, let's go kick some Thorpe butt!" Autumn called out and grabbed her duffel bag.

Kiera followed reluctantly, wishing she could go back to her office and hide out for a while longer. Her breakfast last weekend with Axel was sticking in her mind though. He'd been so clear about his desire, she was nervous about being around him again.

And then there were the few times recently he'd walked by her office and caught her at odd hours. He'd walked by just last night around ten o'clock and paused in his stunning tuxedo, the bow tie hanging down around his neck as if he'd just come from some glamorous function near the office, which was probably the case since the Thorpe brothers worked the social circuit just like any other business owner would. But that day he'd shaken his head when he'd seen her. He'd also caught her here early in the morning and several more times late at night. His expression indicated that he thought she didn't do anything other than work. As she remembered his disapproving face that night, she squared her shoulders and followed Autumn. She'd show him!

Fifteen minutes later, the sun was beating down on her hat and the two teams were trash talking as Axel and Ash flipped a coin to see who would be up to bat first. Unfortunately, Axel lost the coin toss. He came over to the team and started calling out field assignments. When he was done, she stood alone while everyone else ran out to their positions.

"What about me?" she asked, standing up to Axel as her anger increased.

Axel looked out at the field and she couldn't see his eyes at all because of his dark sunglasses. "Why don't you sit this inning out?" he suggested. "I'll get you out there soon." He watched her pale skin suffuse with pink which he knew wasn't a blush but a sure sign that she was angry with him. Unfortunately, he was thinking about how cute she looked in those short shorts and the way her freckles stood out a bit more when she was angry. He also didn't want her pale skin to get burned out here in the abnormally hot sun. It might be fall here and the weather cooling down, but skin like hers would probably burn at the first touch of sunshine.

Besides, he didn't want the other guys on the team, or the men in the stands, to see her butt in those shorts. They were too short, he thought. His imagination was going wild, wondering what kind of underwear she was wearing underneath those shorts. He never should have taken off that dress last weekend, he told himself. He wouldn't be able to handle her bending over when she was up to bat. Nor would he be able to tear his eyes away from her if she were out on the field.

There was also the possibility that she would embarrass herself by missing the ball or striking out. He liked playing ball, but Kiera probably didn't even know how to hold the bat much less hit or catch the ball when it came at her.

Kiera thought about arguing with him, but he obviously knew the other players, their strengths and weaknesses better so she walked stiffly over to the bench and sat down with a thunk. If they'd had a few practices, she might have been able to show him that she wasn't a novice at softball. She loved the sport and had played in high school. Admittedly, she hadn't done much in the past few years but she'd caught a few games with friends in San Francisco. Crossing her arms over her chest and leaning back against the dugout wall, she watched through her own sunglasses, feeling smug since she got to watch Axel as he walked around, coaching the other players. It gave her a nice view of his very tempting butt and deliciously broad shoulders.

After the first inning, she had to accept that he was a pretty good coach. He didn't step in when he wasn't needed and he simply laughed when someone got out. He recognized that this was a competition, but not a win or die game. It was just a fun, social game that everyone pushed to win, but they weren't going to lose anything if they lost.

The only thing that really infuriated her was that he didn't put her in any of the field positions and he didn't let her go up to bat. She kept telling herself to be patient, that he didn't know she could actually play softball. It had never come up in their conversations all those years ago, so he had no clue that she was actually a pretty good hitter.

When the sixth inning arrived and left, she'd had enough. "Put me up to bat, Axel," she demanded, glaring up at him through her sunglasses. He didn't need to see her eyes to know she was angry.

Axel stared down at her, worried about embarrassing her. He mentally debated back and forth with himself. All of her co-workers were out there and if she messed up or struck out, she'd be hearing about it for the next week. He'd known she was on the team and he should have brought her out here to the park earlier in the week to see what she could do, but he'd been tied up in court. And he hadn't been sure he could keep his hands off of her, to be perfectly honest. Even now, looking at her long, sexy legs in those shorts was driving him more than a little nuts. She might be wearing a sports bra under the softball shirt, but that didn't help him a lot in dealing with the need to pull that shirt up over her head and free her perfect breasts from the confines of the merciless bra.

Focus, man! He'd told himself that over and over this past week. He'd seen her so often in the office and he'd been trying to figure out a reason to get her alone, but she was always working.

He sighed and looked around at the other players. Some were watching him, wondering what he was going to do. He had to put her in or everyone would be talking about her lack of game time tomorrow as well. He was dammed if he did and dammed if he didn't. "Are you sure you want to do this?" he asked gently.

Kiera refrained from rolling her eyes. Instead, she just stood there, staring at him and waiting for him to come to his senses.

Axel sighed, pushed his hat back on his head and shook his head. "Look Kiera, I know Autumn roped you into joining the team while you were out to dinner with the ladies last weekend. You don't have to do this," he said calmly.

Again, she didn't say a word, just waited angrily for him to agree to her demand.

"Fine!" he relented, recognizing the stubbornness that made her such a good lawyer. He bent down and picked up a bat. "Stand with your feet apart, bracing just so. Don't choke the bat. Keep your hands like this," he said and showed her how to hold the aluminum bat.

Kiera's irritation grew exponentially as he patronized her. Grabbing the bat, she flipped it around easily so she was holding it at the grip end. Then she poked him in the middle of the chest with the other end. "Back off, buddy!" she snapped. "Just stand there and watch."

There were several yelps from the other team and from the rest of the crowd who had shown up to watch. She didn't look back to gauge Axel's reaction to her prodding but took up her position at home base and signaled to the pitcher that she was ready.

The pitcher, another lawyer in Ryker's group, nodded his head and smiled, thinking this was going to be an easy out. Kiera didn't mind. Let them assume the worst. It would just lower their guard and she'd be able to show them more easily that she wasn't some hothouse flower that needed to be coddled. She hadn't joined the team just to show up and warm the bench. She was a good player, darn him!

She watched carefully, painfully aware of Axel standing right behind her and the length of her shorts. She was pretty sure he was watching her butt instead of her stance, but she pushed that thought out of her mind. She was on a mission and she wasn't going to let his lascivious thoughts impair her....

"Strike one!" the referee called out behind her.

Kiera blinked and looked around. When had the pitcher thrown the ball?

Shoot! Focus girl, she told herself firmly.

She was just about to take up her position again but Axel called a time out.

She turned around and looked at him, silently questioning why he'd stopped the game.

He walked over to her and leaned down. "Just take your time. Watch the ball and when it passes over that point," he explained, pointing to a space a few feet out from home base, "Start your swing. Okay?"

Kiera shook her head. "Axel, I really can do this."

He smiled slightly and she had a moment of panic when it looked like he was going to bend down and kiss her. "I know, honey. Just..." he was at a loss for words and she felt her knees melting with his endearment.

"I promise I know what I'm doing, Axel," she shook her head, saying that more to herself than to him. "Just stand back," she said, looking up at him, almost pleading with him through her eyes that he couldn't see because of her sunglasses. "I can do this. I promise. Have a little faith."

Axel's jaw tightened and he hesitated for only a moment. "Fine," he said and stepped back again.

Axel watched as she stepped back into position and signaled to the pitcher to go ahead. His whole body was tense and worried. He didn't want her to be embarrassed by another strike but.... "Strike two!" the referee called out again.

He bit the inside of his mouth, wishing he'd never put her into the game. It had nothing to do with winning even though they were down by three points and they had three players on base. This was all about making sure she wasn't hurt. The teasing in the office tomorrow could be brutal!

He tried hard to focus on the pitcher, wishing he could give Kiera some sort of signal on when to swing, but he couldn't look at her. His eyes weren't paying attention to the pitcher or even the ball. Not with her adorable, round butt poking back at him.

And then he heard the thwack! He swung back to see what had happened and sure enough, the softball was flying through the air! It wasn't just flying either, it was arching way out and several outfielders on the opposing team were racing to try and intersect with the ball.

He looked at the field and one, two and then three people came over home base! The ball went far and no one was able to connect fast enough so it dropped to the ground. He looked out and his breath caught in his chest as he watched Kiera's gorgeous, long legs racing from first base, then second base. He looked at the ball and suddenly realized that he was supposed to be giving her direction based on where the ball was. "Go to third," he called out, racing over to third base. His eyes flashed from the ball that was now being thrown from one player to the next and then to Kiera who was flying past third base. "Stay there!" he called out.

But did the stubborn woman listen to him? No!

Damn her, she was racing the ball now! The other team was getting the ball and Kiera was flying fast, but was she fast enough? Halfway to home base, the pitcher caught the ball then swung around, throwing as fast as he could to the catcher.

He watched as Kiera caught the other team member pass the ball out of the corner of her eye and, he couldn't believe it, but the woman found a burst of speed and flew by him.

It was close! But Kiera slid through the sand and dirt and Axel watched with amazement as Kiera and the ball flew over the base. Dust was flying everywhere, blocking his view and his heart jumped to his throat as his eyes leapt to watch the referee. When he saw the ref's arms swing outward, indicating that she was "safe", he threw back his head and laughed with the release of tension.

Damn! He walked over to where everyone else on the team had already assembled. Everyone was patting her on the back but Axel was watching her face, seeing the dust settle not just on her but on everyone else around her, all of whom were almost dancing with amazement and glee. Then he noticed something else. Something not good. Someone patted her on the back but the crowd accidentally pushed the person into Kiera's side. It was fast, only a flash, but he caught the cringe when the person bumped against her and he quickly pushed his way through the crowd. Bending low, he saw the scrapes on her leg and the blood that was starting to seep through the thick layer of dust.

"You're hurt!" he growled, ignoring the whoops and hollers of congratulations that were being thrown about.

"I'm fine," she said, grinning from ear to ear, trying to dismiss the concern in his voice. "And I told ya so!" She was too elated to worry about a few scrapes or bruises. She might be in pain later tonight, but for now, she was just reveling in her wonderful I-told-ya-so moment.

Axel was stunned for a long moment, looking down into her gorgeous eyes and shook his head. "Yes, you did," he replied, smiling back at her.

Conscious of everyone in the office congratulating her, he stepped back, not wanting anyone to see how concerned he really was for her but still stunned at the pride swelling up in his chest. She'd won the game for them, he acknowledged with a shake of his head. She'd actually won the game.

"Beers at Durango's!" he called out and everyone cheered and started heading towards the bar that was one block away from the park where they'd played.

A movement to his right caught his eye. He shook his head as he watched Autumn and Xander argue about something. Then to his left, he spotted Ryker and Ash looking smug, both with their arms crossed over their chests as they watched him with an irritating smile.

He thought about going over to demand an explanation, but then saw Kiera again and his brothers were forgotten. Everyone had cleared out quickly with the promise of beer but Kiera was one of the last to grab her bag. And she was limping!

He glanced down at her leg and cursed under his breath. Marching over to her, he was suddenly furious with her for lying to him. "You're hurt!" he growled when he finally reached her.

He bent down and examined the scraps and knew that they were deeper and more painful than she was letting on. "Damn it, Kiera! Why didn't you tell me?"

"Because I knew this would be your reaction!" she yelled right back at him. "Besides, I'm perfectly fine!" Or she would be if he would take his hands off of her leg. Those large, gentle hands were making her stomach flip flop. Not to mention, his brother, her boss, was looking in this direction and she didn't like appearing weak when her boss was around. She had to be sharp and on top of her game. She'd just brought in three players in a game that they could have easily lost, couldn't he stand back and let her have her moment?

On the plus side, she wasn't thinking about the pain in her leg when he was touching her. On the down side, she was thinking about too many other things which were completely taboo when he was touching her.

Axel was having none of that. She could be strong and confident in court. He wasn't going to let her walk on a damaged leg outside of the office. "You're not fine!" he countered and lifted her up into his arms. He ignored her protests and carried her back into the dugout, setting her down gently on the bench.

"I'm fine," she exclaimed when she realized what he was about to do. She tried to wiggle away, to stop his large hand from touching her leg but he simply moved his hand higher up onto her hip so she couldn't move. "Really, I'm fine. It was just a small scratch and I'll put some ice on it when I get home tonight."

Axel was having none of that. "Shut up and let me clean up your leg." He walked over to his bag which contained a first aid kit and grabbed the towel out of his duffel bag. Dunking the towel into the cooler, he came back over and started cleaning her leg.

The towel was now freezing and she cringed at the first touch. "Axel! That's cold!" she said, her breath hissing through her teeth as she tried to pull away. But he just put a hand on her thigh, holding her in place.

"This needs to get cleaned up," he said, focusing only on her leg that was quickly bruising although the bleeding was slowing down. He refused to think about her warm thigh or the way the muscles in her leg flinched under his palm. And he definitely wasn't going to think about how her whole body used to flinch when he would touch her before. Or the way those flinches were usually followed by "Please Axel" or "Hurry Axel!" or she might gasp when she would touch him back, making him flinch and growl with need.

"Fine, but hurry up," she grumbled. She closed her eyes, not wanting to see his dark hand against the lighter skin of her thigh. But a fraction of a second later, her eyes flew open again but she wouldn't look down. Closing her eyes caused her mind to flash several images that were better left un-flashed. Mentally, she couldn't handle those flashes along with his gentle touch right now. He was too close and too big. And it had been way too long since he'd touched her like this.

Axel looked up and caught the blush staining her cheeks. She was remembering those same moments, he realized.

He looked back down at her leg, carefully cleaning the scrapes from all the dirt that had been ground in by her slide into home plate. "You should have stayed on third base," he told her, his voice deeper than normal.

"I made it home and I scored," she countered with a grin. But then he touched a tender spot and she hissed again, her body stiffening with the pain.

Axel's eyes narrowed in frustration over her stubbornness. "I'm taking you to the hospital," Axel said with grim determination.

Kiera quickly shook her head. "You can't take me to the hospital for a cut on my thigh!" she replied, almost laughing except that her leg really was throbbing. The idea of going to the hospital was outrageous though. Doctors in the emergency room had to deal with gunshot wounds, broken limbs and heart attacks. A bruised and scraped thigh didn't even rate on the emergency room 'badness' scale.

"I can and I will," he said, grabbing her duffel and his own a moment before he picked her up in his arms once again.

She grabbed his shoulders only because that was the only thing available to hold onto. "Axel, going to the hospital for a few scrapes and a bruise is silly. I'll just head home and take a warm shower."

"Fine," he said but deposited her in his own luxury car instead of her more practical sedan.

"I can drive myself," she said as she started to get out of the car.

He stopped her by simply putting his hands on her legs and shifting her right back into the passenger seat. "Either I take you home and make sure you take care of this, or I take you to the emergency room and a doctor takes care of it. I don't care which, it's your decision."

Kiera grumbled but knew he wouldn't relent. "Fine, but I can take care of it myself."

Axel slammed her door shut and walked around, calling Ryker on his cell phone. "You're going to have to pick up the tab at the bar. I'm taking Kiera home. Her leg is pretty banged up." He'd ignored the smug expressions on his brothers' faces right after the game and he didn't care if he and Kiera were the only ones not at the bar with the other players. Let them think anything they wanted. He was going to take care of Kiera!

He listened for another moment, then shook his head. "You're an ass," he replied to whatever his oldest brother replied and ended the call.

Slipping into his car, Axel started up the engine and backed out. Five minutes later, he was pulling up at her apartment building and coming around to her side to help her out. They hadn't spoken a word since he'd gotten into the car, Kiera too nervous about being alone with Axel again. It was just like last weekend, but this time, Kiera knew she wouldn't be able to gracefully and confidently walk away from him.

She was too nervous to look him in the eye so she focused only on placing her feet on the asphalt so she didn't fall on her face in front of him. "I can take it from here," she said and stepped out, smothering the grimace when she accidentally banged her leg on the side of his car because she was trying to move too quickly, needing to be away from him.

She was just reaching for her duffel bag when he plucked it out of her hand. In one swift movement, he lifted her into his arms one more time and kicked the car door closed with his foot then walked effortlessly towards the elevators,.

She breathed in slowly, trying to calm her racing heart. "I can walk, you know." And she ignored the other issues that were happening in her body because his arms were around her like this. It felt too wonderful, the memories of other times she'd snuggled in his arms, against his chest just like this racing through her mind.

Axel ignored her and pressed the call button.

"I'm not an invalid, Axel," she said more assertively, wanting desperately to get down from his arms.

Again, he just ignored her.

"You might have congratulated me on winning the game. I helped score four points."

Still, nothing.

When he was standing in front of her apartment door, not sure what to do, she smiled. "Now you're going to have to put me down. My keys are in my purse, which is in my duffel back which is over your shoulder.

Axel contemplated her comment for a moment but in the end, he lowered her feet to the floor and handed her the bag.

Kiera smiled triumphantly and pulled her purse out of her bag, dug in and found her keys. She'd just unlocked her apartment door and was turned around to tell him goodbye when he picked her up in his arms once again and carried her through the doorway.

"Axel put me down!" she commanded, grabbing onto her purse and her bag so it didn't scatter all over the floor.

He ignored her, carrying her through to her bathroom, looking around at her apartment. "You haven't decorated your place," he commented as he put her down on the bathroom counter. When she tried to slip off, he put a hand to her leg, holding her where he wanted her.

"I haven't had a chance yet," she replied, irritated that her body started shivering once again with his touch. She wished she could control her reaction whenever he was around but there wasn't anything she could do to temper her trembling. When he was near, and especially when he was touching her, she was jelly. And trembling, googly-eyed jelly at that.

He went through her bathroom cabinets and Kiera blushed painfully when he discovered all of her feminine products under the bathroom sinks.

"If you tell me what you're looking for, I can tell you where it is," she told him, her face blushing painfully. She hated it when she blushed because her freckles stood out more, making her look ridiculous.

But the man simply closed that one and opened the next, not even blinking an eye at such an obviously personal item. When he found the washcloths, he pulled several out, laying them on the counter before he turned on the bathroom faucet, waiting for the warm water to flow. When it did, he picked up one of the washcloths and wet it before carefully cleaning the rest of her scrapes and scratches.

Kiera had thought that the cold water was difficult to endure, but she was finding she'd been very, very wrong. The warm water against her skin was almost sensuous. Paired with his strong, hot hand and she gasped, looking into his icy, blue eyes. He looked up at her at the same moment and she knew he was feeling it too.

"I'm fine," she whispered, praying that he would just leave and she wouldn't need to find the willpower to resist him. Because she was seriously doubting her ability to do so.

His eyes looked back down at her thigh, but his hands changed, his touch seemed softer somehow. He was still cleaning all the dirt off, but it was more of a caress than anything else. His hand smoothed over her skin, cleaning and exploring, tenderly touching the tortured areas of her skin, his fingertips a light touch, which was even more beguiling.

"You have beautiful skin, Kiera," he said softly, his voice deeper, huskier.

She took a deep breath, wishing it didn't sound so shaky. "I'm too white," she argued, trying to think of anything to get herself out of this, to make him go away before she begged him to stay.

"Tell me you miss what we had together," he demanded, his eyes capturing hers while his fingers continued to trail fire down her leg.

Kiera wished she could deny his command, but the way he was touching her had eliminated all her defenses to him. "I miss it," she replied, trembling now as his fingers moved down to her knee, then her calf.

With those words, he stood up and Kiera was painfully disappointed that he was no longer touching her. But she'd been mistaken in his intentions. He didn't hesitate a moment before he took her head between both of his hands and kissed her, deeply. His kiss caused her to moan with the contact. Her mouth didn't stop him in any way. In fact, she encouraged him in the only way she knew how. She kissed him right back, forgetting that she was supposed to resist him. Forgetting that this job was only a stepping stone and he'd hurt her terribly the last time their careers had diverged.

It was only Axel now. His hands, his mouth, his tongue invading hers and she kissed him right back with every ounce of desire that had been stored up over the past six years for this man. She wanted him and all the remembered pain was hidden at the moment. It was only the desire, sure and strong, that was on her mind now.

His hands pulled her forward on the countertop and Kiera's hands fisted on his shirt, trying to hold on even though her world was tilting precariously. If he were to stop right now, she might just fizzle out in a spark of heat so intense there would be nothing left of her afterwards.

Of course, if he continued, there was the possibility that the same thing could happen. Her only option was to pull herself closer, to mold her body against his. But that didn't help her in any way either. She needed him so desperately she was in pain with that desire. She couldn't wait. Her hands slipped underneath his shirt, feeling the velvet steel of his chest and stomach covered by a light dusting of hair. He was stronger, she realized. Her fingers explored the angles under his shirt, needing to discover all the changes that had occurred over the years but he was pulling at her. She didn't understand and she almost growled when he did something to pull her hands away. But she realized that he was only taking his shirt off, giving her better access and her hands immediately jumped right back to his chest, her eyes following so she could see the changes as well as feel them. Her fingers moved over his skin, finding all those spots she remembered so well that drove him crazy. When they weren't making love, those spots were only ticklish but as soon as their touch heated up, those spots were an instant erogenous zone and she loved every one of them, touching them all and wishing she could send him as far over the edge as she already was.

He growled himself and lifted her up, carrying her into her bedroom and placing her on her bed. "My turn," he said and swiftly, efficiently, pulled the softball shirt up and over her head. He didn't even hesitate, give her time to understand what he was doing before his hands had even released the clasp behind her back to free her breasts. The ugly but effective sports bra was tossed away and his eyes were hot as he looked down at her bare breasts.

"You're beautiful," he groaned before his head bent, lowered to kiss the tip of her breast. Her nipple pebbled underneath his lips and she arched against him, needing his body against hers. She was frantic now, needing him inside her more than she needed oxygen. She wanted him so painfully, felt empty and terrified that he might leave her before he moved inside of her.

Her hands reached down for the snap of his shorts, wanting to feel his erection in her hands, to guide him to her so he could fill her up. Axel was just as desperate and with swift fingers, her shorts and underwear were gone. He lifted himself up and stripped off his clothes before grabbing a condom out of his wallet. He sheathed himself with the protection a moment before he lowered himself down to her again. Just to be certain, he pushed his hips between her knees, his finger sliding inside her heat. The wetness he discovered there almost made him lose control but he closed his eyes and took a moment before grabbing her hands and holding them over her head while he pushed her legs farther apart, sliding into her welcome heat. "Damn you feel good, Kiera," he groaned while he pushed himself deeper, watching her face to make sure he wasn't hurting her in any way.

"Don't stop," she begged when she thought he might be about to pull out of her. He was larger than she remembered him, but he was still filling her up and making her feel whole again. She hadn't felt this since she'd left that day and she couldn't believe how wonderful it felt to be so intimately connected to this man once more.

And then he started moving. His body surged into hers and she lifted her hips, eager to match his passion. Over and over again he slammed into her, both of them panting in a desperate need to fulfill the ache that had been inside each of them for so long.

When Kiera thought she couldn't take anymore, she started to push his hips away but he knew all her tricks and wouldn't let her. He shifted ever so slightly and that was all it took. Kiera flew over the edge into one of the most mind-blowing climaxes she'd ever experienced. She wasn't even aware of Axel finding his own release because she was still throbbing, still seeing stars.

When he finally stopped and pulled her close, she sighed with happiness. "I remember," she whispered, her hand reaching out and touching his shoulders, his back, anything that was part of Axel.

Axel chuckled and nuzzled her hair out of his way with his nose, kissing her neck and that spot behind her ear that never failed to elicit a giggle of delight. It worked even now and he smiled at the memory as well as the present.

He stood up and went to the bathroom and Kiera heard the water running for a moment but she was too content to try and figure out what he was doing. She pulled the sheet over her as her eyes drifted slightly closed.

"Still shy?" he asked, laughing as he slid back into the bed behind her, pulling the sheet away so that his hands could smooth over her skin.

Kiera gasped, but she wasn't sure if it was because he took away the sheet or because he was touching her again and her body, so recently satisfied, was no longer content. She reveled in the fact that just a simple touch from this man had her whole body tensing with renewed desire. Never before had any man ever had this kind of effect on her. Tomorrow, she might regret his ability to control her so easily. But right now, she couldn't do anything but enjoy the whole process over again, but this time at a much slower pace.

CHAPTER 4

Kiera woke up and instantly knew something was wrong. She looked around, feeling the sheets for Axel and finding his side of the bed empty.

She sighed and thought about that for a moment before she opened her eyes, pulling his pillow close but knowing it would be a cold substitute for the man himself. It was probably for the best. She shouldn't have fallen into bed with him again last night. It was wrong and nothing could come of it. They wanted different things in life and she would move on to the next job while he was settled in here in Chicago.

Then she heard a noise in her kitchen and she jerked around, just in time to see Axel coming back into the bedroom.

His eyes quickly moved over her body silhouetted by the sheet she continued to hide herself under. "You never answered my question last night, Kiera," he said, standing at the bottom of her bed and looking down at her.

Kiera looked at him curiously, pushing her curls out of her eyes and sitting up, making sure to keep the sheet over her nakedness. She ignored his raised eyebrow and focused on what he was asking her. Something about a question? She didn't remember any questions. All she remembered was the incredible, wonderful heat of him as he held her close throughout the night. Even though he'd woken her up several times during the night, she hadn't slept so well since....well, for six years.

"What was the question again?" she asked, not fully awake. But even if she were, she wasn't sure she would be able to concentrate. Not with Axel standing there at the end of her bed in only the pair of shorts he'd worn last night to the game and nothing else. All those rippling muscles and broad shoulders were very distracting.

"Why haven't you decorated this place?" he challenged, his hands fisted on his hips.

Kiera leaned back against the pillows, trying to determine what time it was. "Decorating?" She glanced at the clock across the room from her bed. "It's before six o'clock in the morning and you're asking why I haven't decorated my apartment?" She tried to remember what day it was but everything was off kilter at the moment.

He looked across the room as well and smiled slightly. "I guess your inability to wake up to an alarm clock hasn't changed, eh?" he shook his head. "Still need to put it across the room so you'll get up out of bed?"

She blushed, remembering how he would wake her up when she was trying to shut off the alarm clock. He used to laugh and tickle her, then make love to her until they were both panting and wide awake.

She shrugged about her trouble waking up in the morning as if it were normal. "It works for me," she said softly and shifted uncomfortably. "What are you doing?"

He glared at her. "You thought I'd left, hadn't you?" Her blush was all the answer he needed. "Kiera, why haven't you decorated this apartment?" he demanded.

Kiera sighed and looked down at the comforter, pretending like she didn't want him to come right back to bed with her and make love to her one more time. "I just haven't gotten around to it yet."

There was a long silence while she waited tensely for him to respond. She wasn't sure what to say to him, how to explain the barrenness of her living area.

"You're not staying, are you?" he guessed. But it wasn't a question. "You're only here for a little while, just enough time to get The Thorpe Group on your resume before you move on to another job." He watched her carefully and, by the guilty look in her face, knew that he'd guessed accurately.

She looked around, trying to think of some comment that would appease him. But he was right. And she knew she looked guilty.

"How long were you willing to stick it out, Kiera?" he demanded, becoming angry with her lack of forthrightness. "A year? Two years?"

She shrugged slightly. "Why do you care?" She slipped out of bed and grabbed her robe. "And how can you judge me when you were doing the same thing years ago? When we first met, you didn't bother to even unpack some of your things," she countered, referring to the boxes he'd kept in his closet that contained all the things he hadn't needed and so he hadn't bothered to find a place for in his apartment. "Don't judge me for doing the same thing you did."

He was livid with her refusal to understand what they had together. She was purposely being obtuse. "Except the position with the Supreme Court was just that, a temporary position. I went into it knowing that I wouldn't be staying with them."

"So what's wrong with me doing the same thing?" she yelled back at him, feeling defensive at being caught. She wished this conversation hadn't happened, but she wasn't going to lie to him. Besides, of all the people she knew, Axel was the one person she thought would understand.

Axel's hand went through his hair, messing it up with his frustration. "The difference is that my position in Washington, D.C. started out only being a temporary position. A job with The Thorpe Group isn't temporary. Nor do we offer positions to people who think we're just a stepping stone."

That wasn't fair. She had no idea what could happen in the future but he was purposely being stubborn about admitting that anything could happen. "But you have people coming and going all the time. It isn't like The Thorpe Group is a be all and end all for employment."

"It could be for you!" he came right back, furious with her for not investing more in their relationship even though it had only started up again the previous night. "You can't tell me that you thought The Thorpe Group was offering you employment only for a limited time."

She shifted uncomfortably, wishing he weren't so perceptive. But that was one of the reasons she'd fallen in love with him. He was amazingly astute and intelligent and he'd seen things in her that even she hadn't known existed. He thought she was pretty, he liked her freckles and he'd made her laugh at the ridiculous things in life. That didn't help her now though. "No, but that isn't the point."

"What is the point?" He was so furious with her he could barely think straight. She'd come back, but not to him. He'd thought last night...but everything he'd hoped for as he'd made love to her, as he'd held her in his arms last night had been a lie. "Am I just a stepping stone?" he asked with an emotionless tone of voice.

Kiera's neck snapped around, shocked that he would ask that kind of question. "What's that supposed to mean?"

"Am I only your next lover in a long line of stepping stone lovers?"

She gasped. "I haven't ever..." she stopped herself and closed her mouth. "Don't..." she was so hurt that he would think that of her, especially when she hadn't been with any other man besides Axel. All these years she'd dated, but no man had ever made her feel the same kind of intensity that Axel could do to her with just a look. "Get out!" she snapped. She wasn't going to admit that to him. Ever! Let him think the worst of her. He meant nothing. He was just a jerk who thought the worst of everyone!

"Gladly!" he growled back, grabbing his softball shirt and snapping it over his shoulders. He didn't even bother straightening it, just grabbed his shoes and socks and walked out of her apartment.

Kiera watched him leave, furious and hurt and aching, wishing she had the courage to call him back. But what could she explain? He was right. She had accepted this offer and considered it just a stepping stone. All lawyers worked their way from one law firm to another, gaining experience until they had the ability and reputation to open their own law firm or made partner in a firm that was prestigious enough to keep them. The Thorpe Group was the cream of the crop of legal firms in the United States, but that didn't mean something might not come along that would serve her future better. Only a stupid person would go into a job thinking they were there to stay. Things happened, the world changed, opinions shifted and companies were bought and sold.

He was wrong about the way she thought of him though. She never would have thought of him as a temporary lover much less a man who was one in a long line of lovers. She whipped her robe off and marched to the shower, trying to scrub off the touch of him, his scent. But no matter how hard she scrubbed, she couldn't get the incredibly alluring scent of Axel out of her mind.

She hurried to get ready for work, needing something to take her mind off of his hurtful words.

Her thigh ached and she took some ibuprofen, stuffing the bottle into her purse, knowing she would need more later. It was a work day and she didn't have time to waste pining away about a man who had unrealistic expectations of her. And unfair ones!

She was fully dressed once again, feeling protected in her business suit and heels. She had a full day of client meetings today along with strategy meetings. She had several briefings to type up and so many things to do that didn't have anything to do with considering where she would be in a year or two. She definitely didn't have time to mess around with Axel Thorpe and all of his obnoxious assumptions.

At the last minute, she remembered that she'd agreed to meet Autumn, Mia and Cricket after work for a workout. So she ran back and grabbed her yoga gear, slinging the duffel bag over her shoulder before storming out of her apartment. Adding to her irritation this morning, she had to take a cab back to the softball field because of Axel's overly protective actions of the night before. Since he'd insisted on driving her back to her place, she didn't have her car.

She could ask Autumn, Mia and Cricket what she should do, she thought. After their workout, they would go out for dinner and she could explain the situation to them. She thought about Autumn's position in the Thorpe Group and bit her lip in indecision. It might not be a good idea to tell the office manager about this. But then shook her head. Autumn was her friend. They'd shared other things and this would just be one more. She trusted Autumn's advice and knew that her friend could separate herself from the situation and give her an unbiased opinion. Besides, Mia was engaged to one of the other partners and Kiera suspected that there was something going on with Cricket and Ryker. So they were all connected somehow to the owners of the law firm.

As she stepped into the cab and gave the driver directions back to the softball field, she considered her options again from their perspective. Maybe it wasn't such a good idea, she thought as the cab made its way through rush hour traffic. She didn't want to put her friends into an awkward position.

The day was tough but she plowed through her work, getting kudos from several senior lawyers on the briefs she helped them with. But she was relieved when it was finally six o'clock and she could get out of the office. She'd tried to stay in her office and out of sight as much as possible, not wanting to run into Axel today. Her feelings were a bit too raw to see him so she avoided as much contact with her co-workers as possible.

When she walked out with Autumn, she breathed a sigh of relief that she'd successfully avoided Axel all day. As she drove with Autumn to their yoga class, she found out that Axel had been out of the office all day in court. Kiera was so relieved that she took several deep breaths, feeling instantly better.

The four of them changed in the locker rooms of the gym, laughing and joking about the day. Autumn and Mia had been friends for a long time, but Kiera already felt like these three women were her sisters. They'd laughed and dined together and she felt a kinship with them that she'd never felt with her other friends in the past.

Axel had endured a miserable day, irritated with everything. His client hadn't followed his advice so there had been a potential lawsuit over some problems with materials coming into the country. He'd fixed that, but it had required him to drive down to the waterfront, then to the courts again so he could defend his client in front of a judge.

At least the day was over, he thought, rubbing the back of his neck to try and relieve the stress. It might not have been such a horrible day, but the beginning had left him furious with the world in general and one lovely, irritating and stubborn woman in particular.

Axel drove through the evening rush hour, still furious over Kiera's responses this morning. Or her lack of the response he wanted to hear. He couldn't believe she'd curled up against him all night, knowing that she wouldn't be here in a year or two.

How could she react to him like that and all the while, know that she was going to move out of his life? Didn't she realize how precious this thing they shared was? He'd dated other women, of course. But none had ever touched him like she had.

Oh, they might have touched him physically but Kiera struck something deeper, more elemental and he knew that she felt it too.

He hated the idea of her moving on, of another man touching her like he wanted to touch her. He'd had her at his house, in his bed and he was right back to trying to figure out a way to make her want to stay, to live with him forever.

His phone rang and he glanced at the caller. Since it was his brother Ash, he pressed a button on his steering wheel to answer the call. "What's up?" he asked, wondering what Ash might need now that he had Mia in his life. The man was besotted with her. Axel was happy for his brother, but he couldn't deny that there was a large chunk of jealousy that his youngest brother had found the love of his life.

Well, truth be told, Axel had found the love of his life as well. He just hadn't figured out how to convince that stubborn woman to love him back.

"Hey, are you coming back to the office tonight?" Ash asked.

"I'll be there in about thirty minutes," he replied, still distracted by his situation with Kiera. It didn't help that Ash was disgustingly happy with his new fiancée and he was still livid with Kiera.

"Mia's car isn't working properly. I just had someone pick it up and tow it to the shop but can you pick her up from yoga class? It's right on the way from where you probably are right now and the office."

"Sure. Send me the address and I'll bring her to you."

"Thanks bro!" Ash said and hung up.

A moment later, a text came onto his screen and he plugged it into his GPS. It was right on the way, so he didn't even need to alter his route.

Ten minutes later, after parking and walking into the yoga center his brother had sent him to, he was even more furious than he had been when he'd taken his brother's call. He definitely didn't mind picking Mia up. She was sweet and made his brother happy so, as far as he was concerned, Mia was family already. He'd protect her just like he would his brothers.

No, he wasn't angry at the issue of picking up Mia. It was that Mia was in a yoga class with none other than Kiera. And the way Kiera was moving was nothing short of….erotic. He hated using that term to describe a form of physical fitness but the downward dog had Kiera's adorable but going straight up into the air. Axel swallowed painfully as his mind conjured up all the things he wanted to do to Kiera while she was in that position.

Position after position, Axel watched with rapt attention, fixated on Kiera's long legs and round, amazing butt, her strong arms and her slender body. After each movement, he wanted to yell at her for making him hard as a rock but he couldn't speak, could only stare in rapt fascination.

And that was before she arched her back with her legs flat on the floor. She looked like some sort of snake with her face up towards the ceiling.

Axel remembered the expressions on Ash's face as well as Ryker's last night after the softball game. Had his youngest brother set him up? They'd both known, just from the way he was treating Kiera, that she was significant to him. When Kiera moved into yet another yoga pose, he had to tear his eyes away. Either that, or storm into the room, grab her delectable body and carry her off to some place private so he could ravish her.

He stepped away so his voice couldn't be overheard and dialed Ash's number. When his brother answered, the tone in his voice confirmed his suspicions. "You did this on purpose didn't you?" he demanded.

Ash's only response was to laugh through the phone lines. "I don't know what you're talking about. But isn't Kiera in that class as well? I saw her walking out with Autumn earlier and they both looked determined to get out of the office in a hurry."

"You'll pay for this," Axel groaned, watching with fascination as the group stood up, then hung down from the hips with their fingers to the floor. Yet another perfect position for him to observe Kiera's derriere. He turned away. "Why don't you do your matchmaking with Autumn and Xander!" he snapped. "Lord knows something needs to be done about those two before they kill each other."

"What, do I suddenly have a death wish?" Ash asked with amusement.

"Leave me out of this," he barked in the lowest tone his aching body could handle.

He heard a chorus of "Namaste" and snapped his phone off. Turning, he tried to appear casual, but the wary expression of the four women when they saw him told him that his casualness wasn't working.

"What are you doing here?" Kiera demanded, her eyes scowling at him as she confronted him on behalf of her friends.

He looked down into Kiera's eyes, trying to get his body back under control. She stood in front of him with pink cheeks and sweat glistening on every inch of her perfect, pale skin. He took a deep breath, but that didn't help since all he could smell was Kiera's sweet scent and it made him ache even more.

"I'm here to pick up Mia. Ash said he towed your car in for repairs." He spoke to Mia, but his eyes remained on Kiera, noting the sweat glistening on her chest and shoulders where the yoga outfit didn't cover her skin. "Are you ready to go?"

Kiera stepped in front of Mia, shaking her head. "Mia didn't do anything to make you angry. I'll drive her anywhere she needs to go."

Axel was having a hard enough time not pulling her into his arms and kissing her until she didn't have the strength to argue, so her belligerence only sparked his anger hotter. "Kiera, so help me, after this morning, I'm likely to toss you over my shoulder and finish our argument. So just let me get Mia and get out of your way, or prepare for a battle you won't be able to win."

Kiera considered his words, not really sure how to handle him like this. She'd never seen him so furious but she wasn't going to let her friend get into his car. "I'll take…"

"It's okay," Mia said behind her, laying a calming hand on Kiera's shoulder. "If Ash sent him, I'm sure everything is okay."

Kiera thought about that for a moment. "Are you going to behave?" she demanded of Axel, getting angry herself, nervous that he was too angry to drive.

His eyebrows went up at her challenge and he was intrigued that she would even dare him in such a way. "What are you going to do to stop me if I don't?" he challenged, actually stepping closer to her and glaring down at her.

She told herself that she wasn't afraid of him, and fervently hoped that she was faking it well. "I'm not going to let you take Mia."

He almost chuckled at her brave words, noticing the rapid pulse throbbing at the base of her throat. "And you think you're big enough to stop me?" he asked, his voice silky soft and smooth now.

"I think I could take you down," she replied, but the words didn't have any force to them now.

"Everything okay?" a new voice called out to everyone.

The new voice was the instructor who was busy gathering up the next class. Kiera looked over at the kind woman and smiled. "Everything is just great," she said and looked up at Axel. "Isn't it?"

"Great," he replied back at her. "Ready to go Mia?" he asked, still watching Kiera.

Mia smiled and nodded brightly, understanding the underlying tension between these two people. "Very ready," she replied, trying to stifle her laughter as she watched the two combatants try and intimidate each other. Axel was so similar to Ash in this way that she wasn't worried in the least. She knew that Axel wouldn't harm anyone and Mia also knew that Kiera was pining for this man quite urgently herself.

Axel turned and looked at Mia, forcing a smile to his face. "Let's hit it then," he said and put a gentle hand on her arm to lead her out the door.

Mia's smile broadened and she started walking, but right before they reached the door, she turned around and winked at Kiera before running ahead and pushing the doors open to precede Axel.

Kiera watched, furious for some unexplainable reason. When the two of them were out of sight, she turned around with a low growl and started stuffing her towel and yoga matt into her gym bag, trying to ease the anger out of her body. She'd felt so good after her yoga class, then she saw the man who only infuriated her further.

Every time she saw him her emotions became extreme! Why couldn't she just remain calm and unaffected?

Autumn and Cricket had remained back about a foot during the entire confrontation. Even now, they glanced at each other then back at Kiera as she furiously stuffed clothes, yoga mat and water bottle into her gym bag.

"Are you thinking what I'm thinking?" Cricket asked Autumn.

Autumn nodded her head, her eyes wide with surprise. "Pizza?" she suggested to Cricket who immediately agreed. "And ice cream," she added in, just in case.

"Maybe even chocolate," Cricket sighed, completely understanding what Kiera was going through.

Kiera didn't hear the others, but was totally in agreement when they pulled up to a pizza place instead of going back to the office. She ate two pieces before she could even see straight.

CHAPTER 5

Kiera looked outside, sighing as she realized that she was still in the office later than anticipated. But why should she care? It wasn't like she had anything special to do tonight. Mia was going out to dinner with Ash, Autumn had a repair person coming to her townhouse to fix something and Cricket had some mysterious dinner to attend. Kiera was slightly concerned about Cricket since her friend didn't seem to be looking forward to the event, but there wasn't much she could do about it at this point but maybe call her later and make sure she was okay.

She saved her document and shut down her computer, clearing off her desk as best she could so she could start up again first thing in the morning. She sighed miserably, knowing the only thing she had to look forward to was a lonely, depressing apartment and a microwavable dinner or a bowl of cereal.

With a sigh of resignation, she packed up her bag, intending to work on her brief once she got home and could snuggle up into a pair of yoga pants and a soft sweatshirt. The nights were cooler now and she could open her balcony doors and let the night air in. It was a welcome relief from the painfully hot summer heat they'd been experiencing over the past few weeks. It was a sign that the fall really was finally coming and she loved the anticipation of the cooler temperatures.

She'd heard several people talking about a boxing gym that was down the block. She smiled at the idea of learning to box. Yoga was good at relieving stress, but perhaps she could add boxing to the weekly agenda. It was different, probably good cardio and she could work out her aggressions. Maybe she could pretend that her partner or punching bag was Axel!

She grabbed her gym bag and walked out of the building, turning right down the street instead of left to head to the parking garage. She felt better now that she had a new purpose to the evening. There was a skip to her step as she anticipated learning a new skill and getting rid of some of this tension caused by worry over seeing Axel in the hallways.

When she entered the gym, she was surprised at how many people were still there working out. It was noisy with music and lots of people doing their best to kick or punch large, black bags that looked to be painfully heavy. Most of the people there were men, but she saw several females working out as well which was a relief.

"Hi," she said to the clerk. "I wanted to ask about a trial membership."

The man was more than eager to sign her up for a free week of classes. He showed her around, introducing her to the kickboxing instructor and the boxing instructors that were on hand. The gym even had the normal exercise equipment which was an added bonus. She went through to the women's locker room and changed, getting ready for the next kickboxing class which was scheduled to start in ten minutes. She walked out feeling very proud and brave, selected a pair of boxing gloves and stood by, watching the end of the current class.

She was looking around, noting the different boxers in the rings. Over in the far corner, there were two men in particular that looked especially buff and amazingly determined to knock each other out. She didn't realize her feet were taking her closer, but something about the way one of the men was moving or shifting on his feet drew her closer. Peering through the elastic bands that enclosed the boxing ring, she squinted at the two men, one in particular.

As she got closer, she started trembling as her suspicions grew. And sure enough, when she was closer, she recognized Axel. Her mouth dropped open, stunned at the strength behind each punch and jab. The other man was grinning like an idiot and taunting him and she recognized Xander as Axel's opponent. Their heads were almost completely covered by a safety helmet, but she'd recognize Axel anywhere and she couldn't believe how glorious he looked as he and Xander boxed and danced around each other. Their shots were well placed and determined, both men working hard to win.

Kiera didn't realize that others were now watching her as she stared, open mouthed, at the two combatants in the ring. Her hand touched the bands while her eyes remained transfixed on Axel's amazing, bulging and sweaty muscles. Although Xander was no slouch, in her mind, no man had ever compared to Axel in both strength and perfection. He was like a Roman statue, all perfectly toned and tall, looking even more fascinating by the sweat making all that glorious skin glisten in the overhead lights.

What happened next was completely her fault. She was still watching but she must have moved slightly because Axel was suddenly distracted. Just as he looked over in her direction and their eyes caught, Xander's left fist swung out, catching

Axel's jaw. Kiera watched in horror as Axel's head snapped to the right, then his body fell, almost in slow motion, to the mat.

Kiera had no idea how she'd gotten through the ropes so quickly, but by the time she reached him, her own boxing gloves were torn off and thrown to the side in her effort to get to her man.

"No!" she screamed, running towards him, bending down to take his beaten face between her hands. "Are you okay?" she cried, feeling like her stomach was going to toss out everything she'd eaten earlier today. "Speak to me, Axel," she begged, her fingers shaking as she tried to get the helmet off of his head. "Just say something. Anything!"

"I'm okay," she heard him groan. She couldn't believe it, but his groan almost sounded like laughter but that was impossible!

Kiera sobbed out her relief. "Where are you hurt?" she asked, running her hands over his body and his skull in an effort to find out if anything was broken.

"Only my pride, honey," he said, lifting his hand and touching her face gently but his fingers were still wrapped up in the boxing glove so it wasn't a very effective caress. "I'm sorry if you were worried," he said so only she could hear him.

She laughed, shaking her head. "You took a pretty hard fall. I think you should see a doctor."

Axel laughed as well, putting his arm around her shoulder. "No need but you can help me up," he offered.

She wrapped her arm around his waist and lifted, feeling his enormous weight produced from all that height and those muscles. "Let me take you to the emergency room, just to make sure your head is okay."

She heard several chuckles behind him and Axel smiled lightly. "Really, I'm fine except for my pride. I got distracted and Xander took a good swing. It's happened before."

She tilted her head as she looked up at him. "And it really doesn't hurt?" she asked.

He smiled down to her, genuinely touched by her concern. Hell, he'd take several more hits if it got her running to him like she'd just done. "No. There's enough safety equipment. I'm fine, really."

He stood up, but kept his arm around her shoulders. It felt too wonderful having her close again and he forgot, for the moment, all of his anger at her perception of her job, and him, as temporary.

She watched him walk, noting that he wasn't limping and didn't have any trouble weaving or falling into her. "Well, I guess that's a good thing," she grinned, even smiling at Xander as he approached, taking off his helmet. "If it doesn't hurt, that gives me a bit more confidence that I can handle boxing."

"Why is that?" Axel asked, unsnapping his own helmet.

"Because I got a week long pass to try out the gym. I thought it would be fun to try boxing," she explained.

The two men stared at her for a long, suspended moment. When Xander actually took a step back, Kiera looked up and caught Axel's furious expression.

"What?" she asked, glancing back and forth between the two men.

"You will NOT be doing any boxing," Axel almost yelled, thinking he would take apart any man who stepped into the ring with her. He would not allow her to be beaten and punched by anyone.

Kiera stepped back, looking at him strangely. "But you just said that there's a lot of safety equipment and you didn't get hurt. You even went down, almost knocked out, by Xander's last punch."

Xander chuckled as he walked away quickly. Axel, on the other hand, moved so he was standing right in front of her. "Kiera, listen carefully, I will not allow you to take up boxing. It is too dangerous."

She squared her shoulders, not intimidated by him at all. "Oh, so you're saying it's a good enough sport for you, but when a little woman gets into the picture, it's too dangerous?" Her voice was low and ominous.

"It's not too dangerous for me because I've been training for years."

"And yet you still almost got knocked out."

He threw up his hands in frustration. "Will you stop saying that?" he growled, irritated that she kept bringing that up. "I told you. I was distracted."

"By what?"

"By you!" he came right back. He looked around and noticed the other men who were watching, amused by their argument. "Let's get out of here. We don't need to continue being a spectacle for the rest of the gym."

Kiera glanced around as well and saw the other men. She pulled back and stepped out of the boxing ring. "Don't worry," she snapped at him. "I'm in the other class."

"What other class?" he demanded, right behind her.

"Kickboxing," she replied and stepped into the area where there were fifteen or twenty black punching bags hanging down from the ceiling.

The instructor was calling out instructions already and Kiera took up her position, refusing to look at Axel as he glared at her from the sidelines. In the end, he turned and headed towards the men's locker rooms and Kiera took out all of her frustration on the punching bag, irritated that she'd let her feelings for him show. Again!

CHAPTER 6

Axel stormed into her office and closed the door. He'd made up his mind and wasn't in the mood to be interrupted. "We have to talk," he told her, leaning against the doorway.

Kiera looked up at him, not sure she wanted to hear what he had to say to her. "Why?"

"Because I can't keep going on like this."

"Can't?" she asked, confused by what the subject might be. Although she could give it a pretty good guess.

He sighed and ran a hand through his dark hair. "Okay, I don't want to keep on going this way." He started pacing back and forth in her small office while Kiera leaned back in her chair and watched him nervously.

She definitely didn't like where this was going. "What do we have to talk about?" she asked, her stomach tightening with dread because she knew exactly what they should be talking about. Mia, Cricket and Autumn had all told her to do the same thing, but she'd ignored their advice, too afraid to face the possible outcomes of the conversation.

"Our relationship."

She looked down at her desk, not able to maintain eye contact with him. "We can't have a relationship."

"I know you think so, because you're hell bent on getting work experience then getting out of Dodge. But hear me out," he offered. "We're both attracted to each other," he said, bracing his arms on her desk and leaning towards her, daring her to contradict that bold statement.

"I don't…"

"No, don't even try to deny it, Kiera. That wasn't a question. The way we react around each other makes it pretty obvious that the attraction we had for each other is still there no matter how much we want to pretend otherwise."

Kiera could accept that, but she still wasn't sure what his point was. "And you're suggesting…?" She swallowed, too afraid to finish the thought.

When she didn't continue, Axel finished for her. "I'm proposing that we stop ignoring this attraction we have for each other. Why don't we just let it out, ride the wave? We haven't been successful at ignoring it, why not try and let it burn itself out?"

She blinked, surprised at his suggestion. "Burn out?"

"Exactly. Starving the fire hasn't helped. Let's just be together until you feel that you have to move on. When that happens, we'll part ways as friends."

"Friends." She tested the word out, not really liking the idea. She didn't want to be friends with him. She wanted to… "I don't think we would be very good friends." She'd been too hurt the last time they'd parted. How was she going to do it again?

He stood up and shrugged those huge, broad shoulders. "Well, we're obviously not very good at pretending we're not lovers. So something has got to give." He sighed. "People are starting to talk."

That was news to her, but she'd been trying to fly under the radar her first few weeks on the job. "Who is?" she asked, sitting up straight in her chair. Gossip was vicious and could ruin people's careers if it wasn't nipped in the bud.

"I don't know specifically who is gossiping, but people are starting to speculate about our relationship. They saw us at the softball game, then again at the gym."

Her eyes widened with horror. "They can't!"

"They are. And the only way to stop it is to not give them anything to discuss. I figure if we stop trying to ignore each other, then maybe we can work this attraction out of our system and it will burn itself out. The fire between us is too hot. Every time we're together, we're singed from the heat so I suggest we let it flare up. Just like all fires, they eventually run out of fuel. I'm guessing this will be the same between the two of us."

She licked her lips, considering his proposition. "You mean, we intentionally become lovers, just with no hope of any future?" she asked, trying to clarify what he wanted.

Axel hated the sound of that. He definitely wanted a future. With Kiera. But he'd been thinking about it and he couldn't figure out how to avoid running into her in the hallways and office events. Their cases would even be connected at times so they had to do something. "Here's the way I see it," he said. "We both want each other. You have future plans that don't necessarily include Chicago. How am I doing so far?"

Kiera wanted to deny everything but she couldn't. So she remained silent.

His jaw tightened furiously when her silence re-confirmed what he'd already guessed. "That's what I thought. So let's just enjoy each other until one of us decides it is over or you move on. Sound good?"

She started to shake her head.

"So I'll pick you up for dinner tonight and we'll discuss the details." He pushed off of her desk and headed towards the doorway.

Kiera bit her lip, her body shaking with the possibility of becoming Axel's lover once again.

He walked out of her office and disappeared down the hallway. She wasn't sure what to do or think and so she stared at her computer screen for a long time.

She wasn't sure how long she remained frozen there, but she knew she had to get her work done. Ash was expecting this to be finished by the end of the day so it could be filed with the courts. That meant she had to hurry up and meet the five o'clock deadline.

Pushing herself hard, mainly to meet the deadline but with a side benefit of not thinking about Axel's suggestion, she worked mercilessly throughout the rest of the afternoon. By the time she sent the brief off to Ash, her fingers were numb. Whether that was due to the speed and duration at which she had been typing or the sheer terror of facing an evening with Axel, she wasn't sure.

Her phone rang by her elbow and she felt her stomach drop out of her body. She knew that it was Axel calling her even before she looked over at the caller ID. Sure enough, Axel's name showed up and her hand shook as she tried to answer the phone.

Unfortunately, it took her too long to answer it so by the time she picked up the receiver, he had already hung up.

A part of her was relieved that she had a slight reprieve but then her cell phone started ringing and she scrambled to answer that before he hung up and thought she was trying to avoid him. She fumbled with the buttons, her thumbs initially unable to press the answer button but she finally did it and was able to bring the contraption to her ear. "Hello?" she answered.

"You're not avoiding me, are you?" Axel's deep voice asked.

Kiera wasn't sure how to answer. "I'm not sure," she finally replied.

His rumbling chuckle told her that he appreciated her honesty. "Good enough. I'll be down in a moment," he replied.

"Wait!" she gasped, sitting up and looking around to see if anyone else had noticed her outburst. "Can I...maybe we should meet at my place. I'll cook something."

There was silence for a long moment until he finally said, "Meet me at my place. Yours is boring."

Kiera immediately sensed that he wasn't thrilled with her suggestion but she wasn't sure why. There was only one way to find out, she told herself and packed up for the night. She hurried through the lobby and down the stairs, hoping to get out of the building before Axel. Her intent was for others in the office to not see them together. If Axel was right and the other lawyers and office staff were noticing them together, she didn't want to add any fuel to that fire. She had enough fires to deal with.

She exited the building and crossed the parking garage and knew instantly that Axel was there as well. She could feel his eyes on her as she walked to her tiny car. She refused to look at him though. If there was anyone else in the parking lot right now, they would see them looking and speculation would increase. She wasn't sure what she wanted from Axel, or even what he wanted, but her primary goal was to not let others know that they were seeing each other. Why that was the case, she wasn't exactly sure.

She drove out of the parking garage, a shiver running through her as she caught Axel staring at her the whole time. She ignored him and drove out, getting onto the highway that would take her to his place. When she spotted him zoom past her in his sporty car, she sighed and accepted that he really was angry with her. He got in front of her and led the way through the streets. Thankfully the traffic wasn't too heavy by this point and they made it to his place without much incident. It would have been easier to go to her apartment which was closer, but she understood that her place represented something he didn't want to acknowledge.

She pulled in right behind him and got out, leaving her work bag in her car, just bringing in her purse. Again it occurred to her that she wasn't completely sure what Axel wanted of their relationship.

"Glad you could make it," he said as she approached.

Kiera looked up at him, hearing the sarcasm in his voice. "What's going on?" she asked carefully, not wanting to irritate him further, but needing to get in sync with his mindset before going forward with anything.

Axel looked down at the woman that he wanted so badly it was now a constant, physical ache. Perhaps if he hadn't had that one night with her. Or maybe if they'd never met so many years ago, he could have met someone else, someone who might be willing to spend her life with him, share her future and her hopes and dreams.

But none of that had happened. And here he was, wanting to pull her into his arms and carry her up to his bed and never let her out of it. He wanted to show her all that they could be together, know all of her dreams and make them come true.

Unfortunately, all she wanted was a temporary lover. Axel had to accept he was a stepping stone.

Instead of answering her and causing words to get in the way, he moved closer, his hands reaching up to hold her head while he bent low and kissed her, showing her what he wanted. He wanted her. Exclusively, for the rest of his life. He wanted to love her unconditionally and have lots of babies with her, to watch those children grow up and for the two of them to grow old together. He wanted to know what it would be like to see her beautiful skin age with time and her soft, brown hair turn silver as their grandchildren laughed around them.

Instead, he had this one night with her. And perhaps a few more.

He would take it. He would take anything she would give him and savor every moment, every kiss and touch and take those memories out in his mind when he was old and alone to keep him warm on those cold nights that he knew were coming.

When he lifted his head, he felt her soft hands gripping his arms, her lush body pressed against him and he felt an odd sort of victory. At least she couldn't deny that they had this between them. "Come inside," he answered her.

"Are you sure?" she asked.

His only response was to raise his eyebrows and pull her hips closer to his.

She laughed softly, blushing at the obvious answer pressing against her belly. "I guess you're sure."

He pulled back and took her hand, leading her through the house. "Are you hungry?" he asked.

Kiera felt the quiet all around her, but there was also the tension that she remembered from years ago. It never quite left whenever they were together. "I'm starving," she answered, holding his hand tightly and hoping he got the message.

He smiled slightly and led her to his bedroom, kissing her as soon as they reached the top of the landing, pushing her backwards as he slowly eased her to his bed.

Kiera didn't need words any longer. When he kissed her, he communicated extremely well. She followed his lead, demanding right along with him. Touching him everywhere, re-learning his touch and his scent, the way he touched her as well, feeling glorious as they spun out of control. And when he entered her, she knew that she would never feel as whole as she did at this moment. With Axel, the world always seemed perfect. No matter what was going on outside the world, Axel and the way he looked at her or touched her, or just smiled in her direction, made everything right and she was happy.

CHAPTER 7

Kiera rested her chin on her palm as the conversation swirled around her. She didn't even realize that she had a goofy grin on her face as Mia, Cricket and Autumn discussed wedding plans. Mia was throwing a big wedding with all of her neighbors and co-workers invited. They'd all helped her when she was arrested and she wanted to thank them, to show them all how much their loyalty and support meant to her.

Autumn had suggested to Mia that she should get married on the same day that her ex-fiancé was to be sentenced for his fraud and embezzlement charges. But Mia only smiled and waved that idea away. Jeff wasn't in her life any longer. Ash was the only man that was important to her. She didn't care what happened to Jeff. They'd broken up long before he tried to frame her for stealing all that money and then his faked murder. They'd all been disgusted when they'd learned how he'd gotten his blood drawn over several months in order to have enough to fake his own death. That was just repulsive not to mention a waste since there were so many people who needed blood as a life saver. Jeff had been selfish on so many levels, it was hard to figure out which was worse.

Her wedding was three months away now and they were frantically getting things organized. A wedding this size normally took at least a year to pull together but Ash refused to wait that long to marry her. So the wedding would be sooner and he gave Mia an enormous budget to make things happen more quickly.

"What about you?" Mia asked.

Kiera looked around and suddenly realized that all three women were now staring at her. "I'm sorry, I didn't get much sleep last night," she replied, smothering yet another yawn. "What was the question?"

The three other women shared a look which Kiera missed because she was nervously adjusting her napkin on her lap.

Autumn spoke up. "Mia was asking what our ideal wedding would be. She's looking for ideas."

Kiera instantly knew that she wanted to get married in the field behind Axel's house, right at dusk with white lights sparkling underneath the huge, oak tree. She didn't want a large group of people. In fact, she would be perfectly happy with just these three women, a few of her college friends she still kept in touch with and...

She was about to think of Axel's brothers but that would mean that Axel was the groom.

She sighed and shook her head. "Yes, um...I don't know exactly what kind of wedding. But probably..."

"Something in the country?" Cricket suggested with a kind, understanding look.

Kiera smiled and nodded her head. "Yes. Definitely something simple and countryish."

Autumn cleared her throat, all of them knowing what was happening. But until Kiera was ready to discuss it, the other women were trying to be mute on the subject and respect her privacy. "What kind of flowers are you getting Mia?"

Mia looked away from Kiera's longing look and focused on her water. "I haven't really picked out the flowers."

Three women stared at her. "The flowers have to be ordered, honey," Autumn said with a slight sense of urgency. "You have the church and the groom, we have our dresses and you have yours. The reception place, the food, the cake and flowers are all that's left."

"I know," she sighed. "That's why I'm asking you guys. I don't really have a favorite flower. I don't want roses because they are too expensive although I love the way they smell and their elegance. And I don't like orchids."

"Daisies," Kiera stated, then looked up, surprised that she'd even said the word.

Mia's eyes lit up. "I like daisies," she said, considering the idea.

Cricket watched as Kiera's eyes turned worried. She shook her head. "I don't think daisies would go with the dress you chose. Daisies aren't formal enough."

Mia considered that for a moment, then nodded her head. "You're right. I guess I should just head to a florist and ask for advice, but they always seem to just get dollar signs in their heads whenever I tell them who I'm marrying. I hate the way all these vendors act like Ash is their lottery ticket. I don't like it so I was hoping to go in with an idea first, tell them to keep it as simple as possible."

Cricket smiled when Kiera relaxed slightly. "What about if we head to the flower market this Saturday?"

Mia cringed. "Ash is taking me out of town this weekend."

Kiera realized this was a good excuse to get out of Axel's proximity this weekend. They'd been spending a lot of time together lately, laughing and cooking, riding his horses. She was starting to have trouble keeping things uncomplicated. She was falling in love again.

Or had she ever been out of love? Was it possible that she'd only learned to deal with the loneliness of being without Axel after they'd left each other during her college years? Had she been in love with him all this time and just suppressing the emotion?

It was possible. She hadn't been with any other man. All of her dates had left her cold and unmoved. She'd even been irritated that they would dare to touch her.

She sighed, unaware that her friends were staring at her once again.

"Did you hear about Linda coming back last week from vacation?" Autumn asked, changing the subject since it appeared that the previous topic was too painful for Kiera at the moment. She turned to Cricket and Mia, explaining that Linda was one of the lawyers in Ryker's group.

"Was she not supposed to come back?" Cricket asked, trying to pretend disinterest.

"It wasn't that she came back early," Autumn said, rolling her eyes. "It was how she came back. She used to have a pretty nice figure, but now she's a bit more...voluptuous."

Kiera and Cricket both looked down at their modest breasts. It wasn't that their breasts were small, they were just...in proportion to their figures. Autumn and Mia were a bit more endowed.

Mia laughed. "If I were to change anything on me, I'd go for bigger lips. I'd love to be able to pout just like those fashion models."

Autumn chuckled. "I'd like to be taller. But I don't think there's any plastic surgery for that kind of wish."

Kiera was fascinated. "Why on earth would you want to be taller?" she asked, leaning back as their lunch plates were taken away. She'd barely eaten any of her salad, but had pushed it around on the plate as thoughts of Axel swirled through her mind.

Autumn leaned back in her chair and grimaced. "I'd just like to be as tall or taller than one obnoxious, irritating lawyer who seems to think he can boss me around."

Kiera laughed, delighted with her friend's desires, even though they were unrealistic. "I hate to break it to you, but Xander can boss you around." If only those two could figure out that they were hopelessly in love with one another, they would be so happy, Kiera thought.

Autumn's eyes flashed. "I know. And he knows it. But if I were taller, I wouldn't be so..." she thought about it for a moment. "I don't know what it is about him that drives me so crazy but he just irritates me. If I were taller, I don't think he would intimidate me as much."

Kiera recognized the signs in Autumn and Xander's arguing because she and Axel argued just like that whenever they weren't talking about things. Like now, for instance. Axel's temper flared at the slightest issue lately. Until she kissed him each night, they always felt like they were on the verge of a huge argument. And Kiera had no idea how to address the issue since she didn't know what was bothering him.

"What about you?" Cricket asked Kiera.

"What would I change if I could do any plastic surgery?" she laughed. "I don't know. Probably go with Linda's idea and get bigger breasts. It might be nice to be considered bodacious," she said, one hand subconsciously going to her chest. "And you?" she asked Cricket.

Cricket laughed right back. "Oh, it would be no contest. I'd definitely become a brunette. These blond curls make everyone think I'm a complete ditz when they first meet me. Including the head honcho over at your firm. He's the worst! I'm pretty sure he's convinced I'm a complete idiot."

The four women were just about to say something when they were interrupted by a very angry, very large Axel who was bearing down on their table.

"Several things," he growled to the four women who were now staring at him with wide, stunned expressions as he leaned over their table. "First," he turned to Cricket, "Ryker feels many things for you, but I guarantee that he doesn't think of you as an idiot. And I daresay he would be furious with you if you dyed your hair." He turned to Mia and started to say something, but stopped himself and just shook his head. "As for being taller," he said to Autumn, "I can guarantee that topping him in height won't solve the problem." He glared down at Kiera and all of his anger seemed to explode in her direction. "And if I ever hear you say you're going to change anything on your incredibly gorgeous, sexy figure, I think I might have to put you over my knee and..." he stopped himself, his lips compressed as he tried to regain control of his fury. "Just don't even think about changing your breasts, or your legs or lips or your hair!" he growled. "Don't change a damn thing!"

With that, he walked away, dropping several large bills on the leather bill carrier that the waiter was bringing to their table before storming out of the restaurant.

The four women stared at the man's retreating back in stunned silence for a long moment before they turned back to each other. A moment later, they all burst out in shocked laughter.

Axel stormed out of the restaurant and back to the office, so livid he didn't even see his brothers who were walking into the building together.

"Axel?" Ash called out when Axel just walked by them, looking like a thunder cloud.

Axel spun around, more than ready to hit anyone who stopped him. When he realized it was his brothers, his fists relaxed, but not completely. "What's up?" he asked, running a hand through his hair in an effort to calm down.

"Are you okay?" Ryker asked.

Axel took a deep breath, trying to get hold of himself. He nodded, but deep down, he wasn't sure he was okay.

Xander wasn't convinced. "How about if we head over to the gym and you can punch my lights out?" he suggested, knowing that something had been bothering Axel for a couple of weeks now.

Axel thought about it, but shook his head. "I don't think that's a good idea," he came back, fisting his hands on his hips. "Why are you three all out here?" he asked.

Ash laughed and rolled his eyes. "We were trying to find you."

"What's wrong?"

His three brothers looked at each other, then back at Axel. "How about if we all head over to my place and we can discuss it?" Ash suggested.

Axel thought about the work he had piled up on his desk, then remembered Kiera suggesting that she get a breast augmentation and he knew he wouldn't get anything else done today. "Fine," he replied and followed them back out to the parking garage. He let Ash drive him to his house, leaving his car in the parking garage. Once there, he slumped down in Ash's plush leather sofa and took the offered beer, downing almost the whole thing in one swish.

Once he put the bottle down and grabbed another, he looked up, only to realize all three of his brothers were waiting.

"What?" he asked, surprised that they were almost ganging up on him.

"What's going on between you and Kiera?" Ryker asked, taking a swig of his own beer.

Axel rubbed his hand over his face, trying to figure it out for himself. "I don't know."

"Why don't you start from the beginning? How long have you two been seeing each other?" Ash asked.

Axel smiled, realizing that Ash wasn't asking just as a brother but as a boss. He considered all of his employees to be part of a team. Not quite family. They all had enough family, they said. But their teams were close, all of them working together, working together as a cohesive unit. A team couldn't do that without some family-like closeness among peers.

In other words, each of his brothers, himself included, watched out for their workers, stepping in when things were getting tough and ensuring everyone had as much of a work/life balance as possible in their stressful environment.

Seeing Ash standing up for Kiera made him feel better. But only a little. He wanted to have the right to stick up for Kiera but she was pulling away, becoming more and more distant even while the sex between them was getting better, more explosive and addictive. He couldn't imagine a time when she wasn't sleeping next to him. In fact, the nights she insisted on sleeping at her own apartment were the nights he barely slept at all.

"We knew each other over six years ago," Axel finally said. His head was leaning back against the leather sofa and his eyes were closed, so he didn't see the surprise in his brothers' faces, but he could feel it. "Stop looking at me like that," he said, still with his eyes closed.

His brothers all chuckled because they knew each other so well. "Why didn't you say something when I presented her to be hired," Ash asked.

Axel felt one of his brother sit down at the opposite end of the sofa and he peeked out. "What was I supposed to say? 'Don't hire her. She's the woman who broke my heart.'?"

Ryker was leaning against the mantle but Axel caught his eyes widen at that confession. "So she's the one?" he asked, just to clarify. All three of them remembered when Axel had come back from Washington, D.C. He'd been driven, mindlessly pushing harder than necessary to get his division up and running. He'd been a bear to be around and had worked eighteen and twenty hours every day no matter how fast his business was growing.

Axel sighed as he nodded his head. "Yep."

Xander shrugged his shoulders. "So what's the problem?"

Axel leaned forward, holding the cold beer in both his hands. "We met in Washington, D.C. when she was in school and I was finishing up my time clerking at the Supreme Court. By the time I'd met her, more than half the pieces were already in place for me to come back here and start my section of the law firm."

"That was a tough time in your life," Xander said, concern on his face as he watched his brother struggle with the story.

"I was pretty angry with her. And coming on board with you guys, I saw it as if I were starting my own law firm. I didn't want to lean on you two for clients or any other support." He turned to Ash and smiled. "You were doing your own clerkship for a federal judge out in California at the time so you weren't around yet."

Ash nodded, then swung his beer out, indicating Axel should continue the story.

Xander interrupted before he could go on. "Why didn't you just bring her back here with you?" he asked.

Ash laughed and the other three brothers looked at him as if he'd lost his mind. "What's wrong with that suggestion?" Ryker asked.

That made Ash laugh even harder. "You wanted her to give up everything so she could come back here and hang out with you?" Ash asked. He reached out and punched his older brother on the arm.

Axel glared at his brother, but didn't retaliate as he normally would. He was too interested to figure out why Ash had said those words. "That's almost exactly what she said. But I still don't get it. I wanted to marry her."

That surprised all of them but they quickly recovered. "And now?"

"I'd marry her in a heartbeat if she'd have me. But she's only here until the next big assignment comes along."

Ash definitely didn't like that. "Has she said this to you?"

Axel finished off his beer. "Not in so many words, but it's true. So I'm only her boyfriend out of convenience."

There was a long silence before Xander spoke up. "I don't believe that for a minute."

Axel stood up and walked over to the fridge, pulling out four more beers and popping the tops before he came back, handing them out to his brothers but keeping one for himself. "What makes you say that?" he asked when he was sitting down again.

Xander shifted on the huge leather club chair so he could see Axel better. "I've seen the way she looks at you. She's hooked. And if you're too stupid to realize it, then you don't deserve her."

Axel's eyes looked at his older brother, then at Ryker and Ash, both of whom were obviously thinking the same thing. Xander was saying that about Axel and Kiera when he was obviously in love with Autumn? Really?

Axel laughed along with Ryker and Ash, all three of them catching the irony in Xander's statement.

"Okay, fair enough. I've got to figure out how to keep her on my own. But if you've got any advice, please let me know. I've been trying to figure this out for a couple of weeks and so far, it seems that my strategy has only backfired."

The men changed the subject after that and the four men proceeded to get drunk in an effort to lose their problems. Only Ash was sober by the time each of them were finding a bed in his house somewhere. He smiled when the doorbell rang, knowing that his newcomer would be Mia. He didn't let her sleep alone these days and she'd been out to dinner with friends.

"Hello, Handsome," she said as soon as he opened the door.

"Why didn't you use your key?" he asked, pulling her into his arms and kissing her so she couldn't answer him.

"I don't know," she laughed when he'd pulled back slightly. "I guess I'm just not used to it."

"You'd better get used to it," he growled and pulled her into his room. "All my brothers are here, by the way," he warned before he slammed the door to what he now considered their bedroom.

"All of them?" she asked, her eyes wide with surprise.

He answered her while his fingers started taking off her clothes. "All three of them. They're in the other bedrooms. Are you okay with them being here?" he asked before he lifted her up and placed her on the bed.

She laughed but snuggled up to him, not the least bit surprised that he'd taken off all of her clothes as soon as they were alone. She was used to it now. "Just wondering," she said mysteriously.

"Forget about my brothers," Ash said as he bent his head to kiss her. "I have other things to discuss."

Mia was in complete agreement with his agenda and smiled as she wrapped her arms around his neck.

CHAPTER 8

"Axel Thorpe," Axel snapped as he answered the phone.

"Having a bad day, old man?" a familiar voice came back with a chuckle.

"Brett?" Axel asked, thinking this might be his old college buddy.

"At your service," Brett Hanson responded with another jovial laugh.

Axel leaned back in his big leather chair, his frustration with his current situation with Kiera forgotten for a moment. "It's been a while. How have you been?" he asked.

The two men talked for several minutes, catching up on their respective lives. Axel was only slightly jealous that his old friend already had two kids and was madly in love with his wife. He thought about what it would be like to say that about himself and Kiera with their kids entering school. And then he thought about Kiera pregnant with their children and he had a hard time breathing for a moment. Kiera pregnant would possibly be the most beautiful thing in the world. As long as he had sons. He couldn't imagine raising a daughter that might look like Kiera. He had enough problems already. Adding a beautiful teenage daughter and he thought he might just lose it. He pushed that out of his mind, refusing to get caught up in that dream. Kiera didn't want that, he knew. She wanted the career.

Maybe at some point in the future, they could work things out and she would be ready to start a family. If he could hold onto her for that long, he thought. He hadn't talked to her about the issue for a while. Maybe it was time to broach the subject. He wanted her and he was willing to do just about anything to keep her.

Axel re-focused on Brett's voice, hearing about all the strange and wonderful things his wife and children were up to. He made a mental note to try and get back to Washington, D.C. to visit him and his family. Brett was a good guy, having gone into business while Axel studied law. They'd done some crazy things throughout their college years together.

"So what's the call for? Surely you didn't just call me to catch up," Axel asked. "You always have an angle."

Brett laughed. "You've caught me. I heard through the grapevine that someone in your group hired a woman named Kiera Ward. She graduated from Georgetown and I've been hearing that she's just the person I need."

Axel hesitated, not wanting to confirm or deny that Kiera was on staff. "What about her?" As far as he was concerned, Kiera was his. Brett needed to keep his paws off of her. It took Axel several minutes to remember that Brett was madly in love with his wife and Antonia was just as infatuated with him. It still took several more minutes to tamp down the jealousy that rose up.

Brett continued, unaware that his friend was having homicidal thoughts. "I have a position that I think she would be perfect for. It's in Paris, which I know she's fluent in French and she also did some work with an international client I stole out from under Watson and Watson three days ago. They're asking for her to join them in Paris and work through some legal issues they're having." Axel listened as Brett continued to describe the role and the criminal problems the client was having.

Axel felt like his old friend had just slugged him. "Why would you need her on your team?" he asked, gripping the phone so hard he was amazed it didn't break into little pieces. "Kiera is more of a trial lawyer than an organizational lawyer. She's pretty amazing in the courtroom."

"That's what I've heard. And exactly the person I need for the job. Ms. Ward has a reputation for being able to see the small details and make them into big ones that a jury can understand. She's quite the litigator even at such a young age."

"You're right. She's pretty amazing," Axel agreed. But that didn't mean he wanted Brett even within a ten mile radius of his woman.

Brett laughed, trying to keep things jovial. "It's an incredible opportunity for her." Brett went on to give Axel more of the details of the position. As Axel listened, his gut tightened. This was an incredible opportunity for Kiera. She would be a fool to turn it down.

"So what do you say? Any chance you could help me convert her to the dark side?" he teased.

Axel sighed and rubbed his forehead. He wasn't sure how to handle this. If he convinced Kiera to take the job, it would be the end of their relationship. If he didn't bring this to her, he wouldn't ever feel right about them being together. This was the nightmare he'd been dreading but it had come significantly sooner than he'd expected. Hell, she hadn't even been working here for a month!

It was still an awesome opportunity. A part of him was thrilled for her, excited that her work and reputation have paid off. The other part of him wanted to hide her away so no one else would ever discover what a fantastic lawyer she was. "I'll talk to her about it," was all he would commit to at this point.

"Sounds great, buddy!" Brett came back. "I'll talk to you later. And thanks for your help. This would be a huge coup for her career."

Axel hung up and just about slammed his fist against his desk. Standing up, he walked over to the windows, staring out into the gloomy afternoon weather but not really seeing anything. His mind was remembering Kiera as she was last night, in his arms and smiling up at him as she touched different parts of his body, making him want her as much as she wanted him. Every moment in her company was an exploration either of her mind or her body and he wasn't sure which he liked more, making her scream out in passion or arguing with her about legal issues. Both fired his mind like no other woman ever had.

He was pacing back and forth, a plan forming in his mind. He wasn't sure it would work but he had to at least give it a try. He walked up the stairs, for the first time ignoring his staff when they called out to him. He had a mission and he had to work out the details as fast as possible. He didn't want Brett calling Kiera before he had a chance to talk to her first.

There was so much he needed to do before this could actually work, but this was not an opportunity that he would relinquish. Hell, he wasn't even sure if Kiera would go through with the plan. He didn't even know if she would want him to come to Paris with her. There was no doubt in his mind that Kiera would take the job. It was too good of an opportunity for her not to take it. This job was a career maker. Once she'd finished working through this issue in Paris, which he suspected might take two or three years from what Brett had explained, she could basically write her own ticket.

Ash was going to be furious about losing her after such a short period of time. He'd already been singing her praises and her clients, even in the short period she'd been here, had come to rely on her more than anyone had expected. Everything everyone said about Kiera was true. She was a fabulous lawyer. But he'd known she would get there six years ago.

He went up to Ryker's office and paused by his assistant's desk. "Is he in?" he asked Joan who was always cheerful despite Ryker's reputation for being a grump most of the time.

Joan looked up and smiled. "He's just reviewing some files. Go on in."

Axel walked in and stopped in the middle of his brother's office, pacing back and forth while he continued to work the issue through in his mind. He didn't even notice when Ryker put down his papers and watched while Axel paced, his mind figuring out the problems that might come up and solutions to overcome or even circumvent them before they happened.

When Axel didn't say anything for several minutes, Ryker picked up the phone and called Xander. "Better come up. Something is going on. Get Ash on your way, okay?" He listened for a moment, then glanced up at Axel and said, "Yes." The pacing continued and Ryker waited patiently while Axel worked through whatever was going on in his mind. Ryker trusted his brothers so if Axel was in here pacing, this was monumental.

A few minutes later, Ash and Xander stepped into Ryker's office, only to see the same thing Ryker had been witnessing for several minutes. They came inside and closed the door, assuming correctly that this was probably a conversation that was better left to just the four of them. All of them glanced at each other, their eyes communicating their suspicion that it had to do with the issue they'd been discussing a few nights ago.

"What's going on?" Xander asked, always the first one to step into any confrontation or issue. Except in one area, that is. And all three of Xander's brothers wished he would face up to his romantic issues with Autumn but none were brave enough to demand it.

"No clue," Ryker replied, leaning his head back against his large, leather chair, waiting for Axel to explain.

Axel turned at the noise and looked around, relieved that his other brothers were here now. "I have a problem," he said. He turned to face Ash. "I'm still in love with Kiera and I can't let her get away from me for another six years."

Ash grinned. "And what are you going to do about Kiera?"

Axel wasn't surprised. Ash would know that this wasn't an arbitrary liaison that would cause problems later on with the proximity of one worker being involved, even formerly, with another staff member. "Thanks. I know we discussed this the other night but now I'm going to do something, or at least I hope she'll let me do something, to make our relationship permanent."

Xander shook his head, relieved that his brother was going to finally do something about the woman he obviously loved. "It's about time!" he teased.

"That's rich," Ash said under his breath. But when Xander turned to face his brother, Ryker stepped in and brought them back to the original issue before things got out of hand. They weren't at the gym with an open space and he didn't relish his furniture being turned into toothpicks by one of his brothers' epic fights. "Are you announcing your engagement?" he asked.

Axel ran a frustrated hand over his face and shook his head. "I'd like to but I doubt she'd accept. Like I mentioned the other night, she's not here for long," he explained. "And what's worse, I just got a call from an old college buddy. He has a fantastic position he wants to offer Kiera."

Ash was already shaking his head. "He can't have her. She just got here and she's already one of the best lawyers I've had on my team. She's smart and funny and the clients love her. It doesn't hurt that she's nice to look at either."

Axel almost leapt across the room at Ash but Xander knew exactly what was about to happen and stepped in at just the right moment to stop the beating. "Not now!" he commanded, holding Axel's shoulders while Ryker stood up and came around to the other side of his desk.

"Ash is right," Ryker said. "Even I've been impressed with Kiera's work. Question is, what are you going to do to keep her on the team?"

Axel turned away and started his pacing. "I can't stop her," he said and all of his brothers heard the pained emotion in Axel's voice. "This really is a great opportunity. She can't turn it down." He took a deep breath and closed his eyes. "This is the same thing that happened in Washington, D.C. but in reverse. Back then, I had the great job I was moving off to and she had to stay put. Now she's got the great opportunity and I'm here in Chicago."

None of them pointed out that he shouldn't consider himself "stuck" when he was one of the managing partners in one of the most reputable law firms in the country. "That was years ago."

Axel nodded. "I know. And I'm not going to make the same mistake I made last time. I lost her back then because I was being a selfish jerk. I didn't understand back then, but I do now and I can't lose her this time."

All three brothers stood shoulder to shoulder, bracing for whatever Axel was about to tell them.

Axel took a long breath, steadying himself for what he was about to say. He didn't want to leave Chicago and his brothers. But Kiera was more important now. Besides, he could fly back and forth to see his brothers. Not having Kiera in his life would be like severing a limb. She was that essential to him now. She had been six years ago, but he hadn't understood all of it then. He wouldn't be so stupid as to lose her this time around. "I'd like to start up a branch of The Thorpe Group in Paris."

"France?" Ash clarified, stunned into saying something obviously stupid.

Axel nodded even while Xander smacked him on the back of the head for being so dense. "Of course Paris, France, you idiot."

That reminded Axel of the conversation he'd overheard recently. Turning to Ryker he said, "Cricket Fairchild is planning to dye her hair brown," he said and waited for the explosion.

"What?" Ryker demanded, his whole body tensing with fury at the idea. "Why the hell would she do that?"

Axel grinned, feeling relief for a moment now that someone else had problems other than him. They'd come back to him, but at least for a few moments, someone else was confused. "Because she thinks that you think she's an idiot. She says that being a brunette would help her disperse that perception."

Ryker rolled his eyes. "Of all the ridiculous…" he stopped himself and took a deep breath. "I'll deal with Cricket. What about Paris?"

Axel wasn't finished. "Oh, and Mia wants roses at her wedding but she doesn't want you to have to pay for them. She's trying to keep the cost of her wedding down since she can't pay for it and you've already offered to do that."

The four brothers stared at each other before bursting out with laughter. When they'd calmed down, Ash nodded his head. "Thanks for the head's up. I'll talk to her."

Axel was about to say something to Xander, but stopped. "Never mind," he said and turned away.

"What?" Xander demanded, stepping in front of Ryker and Ash.

Axel wished he hadn't said anything. But since it was out there, he took a deep breath and said, "Autumn wants to be taller so she can take you down and won't be intimidated when you and she fight. Which seems to be all the time lately."

Xander just stared for a long moment, unaware of the tension that statement had unleashed in the room. Ryker and Ash slowly moved back, knowing that Xander tended to lash out whenever Autumn's name came up lately.

Shockingly, Xander didn't say a word. He didn't get angry or explode in any way. He simply nodded his head and crossed his arms over his chest. "I'll take care of it," he said softly but with vehemence. "Anything else?"

Axel turned back to Ash and chuckled. "Mia said something about wanting fatter lips. I have no clue what that was about."

Ash laughed again. "I'll make sure her lips look…" he stopped and grinned. "Never mind."

The other brothers turned back to Axel, all silently asking him if there was anything else they should know about.

"That's it," Axel confirmed. "Oh, wait," he said, remembering one more thing. "Apparently Linda Sanders got a boob job to try and catch your attention," he told Ryker with an evil grin. "Cricket doesn't approve of Linda's efforts to turn you eye."

Ryker looked confused for a moment. "Linda Sanders? She just came back from sick leave, didn't she?"

Axel chuckled. "Apparently, she had cosmetic surgery."

Ryker still didn't understand. "She looks the same to me." He shrugged his shoulders.

"How did you hear all of this?" Ash asked.

Axel smiled as he remembered the lunch he'd overheard. "I was eavesdropping during my lunch meeting with Phil Matthews last week. They were at a table nearby. The subject of Linda's boob job came up and they all started considering cosmetic or physical changes they would make to themselves. It was interesting to say the least."

"What would Kiera do?" Xander asked, laughing at the idea. He wished he could do a bit of eavesdropping himself.

"Boob job again."

The three other men were surprised. "I know!" Axel said, shaking his head as if he couldn't figure out why she would consider something like that. Then he glared at his brothers because he's just realized that they also considered her figure pretty awesome, which meant they'd been looking at her.

"We're guys!" Xander said in reaction as if that were explanation enough.

"Don't let it happen again!" he growled and all three of his brothers laughed.

As usual, Ryker was the first to get them back to business. "In any case, what are your plans for Paris?"

Axel sighed and started pacing again. "I'm not sure of all the details yet. The only thing I know about is that I'm in love with Kiera Ward and I believe she's in love with me. But she loved me before and she wasn't going to give up her career to be with me. I won't give up my career, but I'll definitely give up my office if it means I get to keep her in my life."

"So you're going to give up your department for her?" Xander asked, not completely understanding but he was starting to get an inkling of what was going on.

Axel didn't hesitate to answer. "I won't lose her again," he replied. "I left her before to start up my department. If it means giving it up and moving with her, I'm going to do it."

Ryker stared at his younger brother for a long moment. "I have several clients in Paris. I'm sure expanding internationally will help me with my group as well."

Xander spoke up with his own input. "And I had a potential client I just turned down yesterday because we don't have a presence in Europe. If you set up a branch there, we could keep some of those clients as well."

"It's tricky," Ash added, "but doable."

Axel's shoulders relaxed. He should have known that his brothers would support him. The four of them always had each other's backs. There was just the four of them, and now Mia. And hopefully Kiera.

"I guess I'd better go try and convince her to take this job then," he said. He didn't want to go to Paris. He loved his house and he loved being with his brothers. But he loved Kiera more. He'd let her go the last time but he didn't think he would survive losing her again. There was so much more to her and he wanted to know every aspect of her.

"You'd better brush up on your French," Xander said, slapping Axel's back.

Ash shook his head. "It's only a twelve hour flight from here to Paris. We'll see each other often. So you'd better get a big place in Paris. Mia will be shopping there all the time. I'll make sure of it."

Axel laughed, truly grateful for such amazing brothers. "Deal!"

He walked out of Ryker's office, feeling better than he had in weeks. He had a plan and he was damn well going to convince Kiera that it would work out this time. He knew she loved him. It was just a matter of getting her to admit it to him. And probably to herself as well, and then working through all the little details that living together created. They could make it though. They had a lot more going for them than many other couples.

Axel walked down the stairs once again, stopping on Ash's floor instead of heading down yet another flight of stairs to his own domain. Now that he'd made the decision and gotten the support of his brothers, he didn't want to wait until later tonight to get her thinking about his idea. He made his way through the chaos that was always present when a team of lawyers worked together on a case. In some cases, when the stress levels were high or a deadline was imminent, lawyers and investigators shouted ideas to each other or rushed papers from one person to another or to one drop off point in a rush to a judge's chambers. He heard it all but ignored the noise, moved around the people rushing through the hallways, stopping only when he reached Kiera's door.

He found her staring out her window, just as he'd been doing about an hour ago. "Got a minute?" he asked, stepping inside and closing her door, leaning against it so he could watch her carefully. He caught the surprised look in her pretty, brown eyes and wished he knew what she was thinking. When she was happy or excited, he could see that clearly but all other times, she hid her emotions well. Maybe, if she gave him the chance, he'd be able to read her in fifty or sixty years.

Kiera spun around, drinking in the sight of Axel with all of his commanding presence and incredible shoulders that she'd come to know so intimately over the past couple of weeks. She couldn't believe that she'd actually thought she could ignore this man. He was just too domineering and handsome for that to have been a realistic plan. What hope could she have had? When the man wanted something, he went after it with a single minded purpose. And he'd told her what he wanted from her that very first weekend when she'd woken up in his bed.

She smiled, thinking of how terrified she'd been that morning, worried about being in his arms and what it might imply for the future. Now she knew, Kiera thought.

With a sigh, she accepted the truth about her feelings for this man. No, she hadn't fallen out of love with him. She'd just learned to smother the pain of not being with him. And six years ago, she'd convinced herself that not following him had been the right thing to do.

Oh, she'd been so so wrong! Falling in love with Axel Thorpe had been the beginning of the end of her independence. She might still be going after the dream, but Kiera knew that the dream wouldn't be complete without Axel Thorpe in it, holding hands with her, laughing and arguing with her and just generally being the man of her dreams.

She loved him so much it almost overwhelmed her.

"Here's the deal," he said and pushed away from the doorway to come into her office, making everything seem smaller somehow. It was only a fraction of the size of his own office, but she didn't mind. It kept her close to him. "I got a call from a guy named Brett that I know from college. He told me about a job in Paris that he thinks would be perfect for you," he explained, his stomach clenching with the smile that appeared on her beautiful face. "I think you should take the job." He ignored her surprise. "But here's the deal." He waited a moment, wondering what her reaction to his "deal" might be. Would she laugh and tell him he couldn't come with her? Or would she kindly accept his presence? Then he shook his head, remembering waking up with her arms wrapped around him this morning. He dove right into it by saying, "I'm coming with you. I've already spoken to my brothers and we've all agreed that it would be a good idea to open up a branch of The Thorpe Group in Europe. Paris could be the first stop and I'll head it up." He crossed his arms over his chest and looked down at her. "We already have ideas for potential clients. And Ash says Mia will be over to shop in the stores as soon as we're settled."

Kiera was shaking her head. "You'll hate Paris," she said softly. She stood up and came around her desk so she was right in front of him and, more importantly, closer to him. She stopped when they were face to face, or more accurately, face to chest since he was so much taller than she was. With a sigh of happiness, she reached up and kissed him lightly. "Your brothers will hate you not being here in Chicago."

Axel's eyes darkened. "Kiera, you're not getting this. I love you," he said with absolute conviction. "And you love me. We're not going through the same thing we did years ago." He put his hands on her shoulders, shaking her slightly to emphasize his point.

"I agree," she said, her smile broadening.

The relief he felt at her words loosened up the band that had been squeezing his chest. "Then call this guy," he said and pulled a piece of paper out of his shirt pocket, "and ask him about the job in Paris. It's a perfect opportunity."

Kiera glanced at the paper, then tossed it onto her desk without interest.

Axel looked down at the paper that had floated off of her desk to the floor, then down at her. "You'll call him later?" he asked, trying to figure her out. She wasn't making any sense. Why wasn't she running around her desk and eagerly dialing the number he'd just given her? It wasn't like her to procrastinate about anything. She dove right into every situation, handling the problems with finesse and class.

She laughed at his confusion. "Nope."

He wasn't sure what was going on. "Kiera, why are you being so vague?"

She laughed softly and reached up again, kissing him one more time. "I've already turned down the job."

That was unexpected. "You've already spoken to him?"

"About an hour ago."

Axel cursed Brett under his breath. "That lying, conniving…" He shook his head and pulled her closer. "You're going to accept the job. It's a great job."

She grabbed onto his tie and pulled, bringing his head lower. She lifted up one more time and kissed him gently, but with more feeling this time. "I'm not taking the job," she whispered against his lips. "And we're not moving out of Chicago."

Axel would have argued further, but he couldn't speak while he was kissing her. "I love you," he told her several minutes later when they came up for air.

Her smile widened and she looked up at him with all the love she had for this man in her eyes. "I love you too!" she laughed, delighted that things were working out so well. Her life might not be what she'd hoped, but thankfully, it was turning out to be even better!

He turned serious all of a sudden and Kiera's smile faded. "What's wrong?" she asked, unaware that her hands were gripping his arms more tightly.

He sighed and ran his hand up her back as if he needed to make sure she was still here with him. "I don't want this to be temporary."

"I don't either," she replied, not sure why he would think anything like that.

"I want to marry you, Kiera. I want to know that every day, you're going to be there by my side. I don't want to worry that you're going to get another job offer and I might lose you."

Was that all he was worried about? She moved closer, snuggling against his broad, muscular chest, reveling in his strength. "Hopefully I'll have a place here at The Thorpe Group for at least a few years. Until we decide to…."

"To what?" Axel demanded, pulling back slightly but not letting her get away from him. "I mean it. I want the whole thing. I want you forever."

She laughed and kissed the middle of his chest. "Until we decide to have kids," she explained shyly. And then something occurred to her. "You do want to have kids, don't you?" she asked, suddenly worried.

Axel let his breath out in a whoosh, relieved that she wasn't thinking of leaving him in a few years. "Of course I want to have kids. With you! Lots of them. And I want to practice making kids a whole lot more right at the moment," he told her, lifting her up onto her desk and pushing her back so she had to hang onto his shoulders to steady herself. "I want you completely at my mercy as well," he said, nibbling at her neck and enjoying her laughter.

There was a knock on her door and, before Axel could give the person permission to enter, they were already coming into the office.

Axel turned to snap at whoever had been so rude but stopped when he saw his frowning brother Ash standing there in the doorway.

"What do you want?" Axel demanded, keeping Kiera in his arms even while she struggled to sit up. She was more than a little embarrassed to have her boss see her in this kind of a compromising position.

"So it's going to happen?" Ash asked, his eyes taking in his best lawyer in his brother's arms. "You're off to Paris?"

Kiera was trying to stand up and look professional in front of her boss, but Axel was making it very difficult. "Um…no…we're uh…" She couldn't get his hands off of her waist to pull her suit jacket down properly no matter how many times she batted his hands away.

"Yes. She's taking the job."

"No. We're staying here."

Axel turned to glare down at her. "You're taking the job. I'm opening up a branch of the firm in Paris. We can be there next month and I can start laying the ground work."

She smiled up at him, already shaking her head. "We're staying here and I'm going to become your brother's most brilliant lawyer," she countered.

"I'm all for that," Ash stated firmly, crossing his arms over his large chest.

Axel sighed. "You're taking the job. It is a fantastic opportunity and you'll regret it later on. You'll resent me for not getting you to Paris. You can be back here in two or three years and we can work through the issues later."

She grinned up at him, thinking she had the trump cards. "I was kind of hoping to be pregnant in two or three years. Maybe even with our second child."

The picture of Kiera pregnant caused a lump to form in his throat and he had to swallow, several times, to be able to even speak. And even then, he wasn't very coherent.

While Axel tried to think of a response, she turned to her boss. "Did you need me for something?" she asked.

Ash was grinning like an idiot but at her question, he snapped out of it and remembered what he'd come in here for. "Yes." He jerked up again and handed her a small piece of paper. "Here," he said. "I'm marrying Mia next weekend. She says you already have the dress to be one of her bridesmaids."

Axel finally found his voice. He pulled Kiera back so his arm was around her waist protectively. "I thought you were getting married in three months. What happened to that plan?"

Ash shook his head as if he still couldn't believe what he'd found out. "I realized that Mia was delaying the wedding so she could get better prices on the food and cake and such. So I called up all of the people she'd worked with and told them to get everything done in one week versus three months and I'd double the amount already agreed upon."

Kiera gasped, her hand flying over her mouth in shock. "Does Mia know about this?" she asked.

Ash laughed. "She does now. We fought about it on the phone but I won." He winked at Kiera. "Mostly because she wants to be married as well anyway so she was only uncomfortable about the money."

Axel chuckled at the idea of his almost sister-in-law being so frugal. It made him feel even better about her joining the family. "At least she isn't after you for your money."

Ash grinned right back at him. "Just my body," he said before he turned and left. He was just about to close the door again but he stopped and said, "By the way, stop molesting my team members during work hours."

"Get out of here," Axel ordered, looking around to throw something at his brother who simply pulled the door closed while laughing uproariously.

"He's right," Kiera said, trying to pull out of his arms.

Axel was having none of that. He'd waited six years for this woman to be his and he wasn't going to listen to anyone telling him he couldn't touch her whenever he wanted to. "We'll fix everyone's perception quickly," he said and took her hand, pulling her out the door.

"Where are we going?" she asked, almost running to try and keep up with him.

"You'll see," he said and stopped in front of the elevator. She pulled her hand out of his since there were so many people waiting there as well.

No matter how many times she asked, he wouldn't tell her where they were going but simply pulled her out of the building and down the street. When they were in front of one of the most exclusive jewelry store in Chicago, she pulled back, shaking her head. "We can't go in there!" she gasped, horrified at what he was thinking.

"Of course we can. I want a ring on your finger so there isn't any confusion. We can't make out in the hallways if people think we're just having an affair," he told her, pulling her close and biting her earlobe.

She laughed and tried to pull out of his arms, but he wouldn't let her and the effort was only halfhearted anyway. "I will definitely marry you, but I don't need a diamond ring to show everyone that. Let's just get married," she said earnestly.

He looked down at her and shook his head. "We're getting married in my backyard, in the field with my brothers and your friends around us. We'll have the wedding reception under that old oak tree with lights going throughout all the branches and champagne to toast our new life together. And there will be daisies everywhere."

Kiera's mind was whirling with shock and surprise. "How did you…"

"I heard you talk about it that day over lunch," he said, his hand moving up to caress her cheek gently. "I want it all, Kiera. I want you, the wedding under the tree, the celebration and the kids."

She didn't realize that a tear had escaped her eyes until he caught the tear with his finger. "I screwed up royally the last time. It caused us to lose six years together. So would you please allow me to do it right this time?" he asked softly but with feeling.

She couldn't believe what a wonderful man he was. "Okay," she whispered back, not able to speak too loudly over the rapid beating of her heart.

"Good. Come on," he said and pulled her into the jewelry store. Ten minutes later, they were walking out again and Axel stopped her right on the street and kissed her, showing her and everyone around how much he loved her. "Now I'm going to call your boss and tell him that you're playing hookie today so I can take you to your apartment and move every box out to my place."

She grinned. "Should be pretty easy since I've barely unpacked."

He rolled his eyes. "There are some advantages to your crazy mindset," he told her and pulled her closer.

EPILOGUE

"Are you..." Axel stopped a few steps into their bedroom, his eyes surveying Kiera in stunned silence.

Kiera turned around nervously, smoothing the satin dress over her curves. "Does it look okay?" she asked, her fingers twitching with the low neckline. "It isn't too..."

Axel suddenly found his voice and looked down at her. "It isn't 'too' anything," he replied, a grin forming on his handsome features. "In fact, I think I might just have to miss my own brother's wedding!"

Kiera laughed, relieved that she didn't look horrible in the dress. It was a lovely shade of blue but the neckline plunged, not so low that it was indecent, but it showed a great deal of cleavage. The rest of the satin hugged her body, cinching around the waistline and hugging her hips and bottom.

Axel came over and reached for her.

"No! You can't touch me," she said and took a step back. "You might stain the dress!"

Axel laughed and grabbed her anyway. "Who chose this dress?" he asked as his hands smoothed over Kiera's hips and bottom before sliding upwards.

Kiera closed her eyes, sighing with the desire now surging through her. "Mia of course. She said she saw the dresses and instantly knew they were perfect."

Axel bent low to nuzzle her neck, enjoying the way her curls tickled his nose. "I fully approve," he commented as his fingers moved up higher, tracing the neckline. He suddenly stopped and lifted his head. "Are Cricket and Autumn wearing the same dress?" he asked sharply.

Kiera had been intent on his fingers and the way his mouth felt against her neck so she didn't understand the question at first. She had to blink several times before she could figure out what he'd just said. "Similar, but slightly different. Why?"

Axel wasn't able to answer immediately because he was too busy laughing. He was laughing so hard he was bent over, holding himself against the dresser, half of which was now hers since she'd moved in.

Kiera stood there, arms crossed over her stomach as she waited for him to regain control of himself. In the meantime, she surveyed his fabulous physique in the tailored tuxedo, reveling in how amazing he looked in the elegant attire. The man wore clothes exceptionally well, she thought. No matter what he pulled on, or off, she was always amazed at how hot he looked.

When his laughter slowed to a chuckle, she raised her eyebrows at him in silent question.

"I think my almost-sister-in-law is doing some matchmaking. And boy am I glad that I was already smart enough to get you before you showed up in that dress," he explained, chuckling again as he imagined his brothers when they got their first look at Cricket and Autumn in this dress. "Xander in particular is going to be furious."

Kiera immediately understood and was amused. "You think Mia chose this dress to spur Xander to do something about his attraction to Autumn?"

Axel nodded, his eyes alight with suppressed laughter. "And I think there's something going on between Cricket and Ryker as well." He led her down the stairs and out to the garage.

Kiera agreed with him. "I think Cricket is great. She and Ryker will make a fantastic couple if they can ever work things out. Although I can't completely figure out what's going on with them. There's definitely some strange vibes happening."

"What kind of strange vibes?" Axel asked, holding her hand while she stepped carefully into his black sports car.

Kiera shrugged. "I can't really put a finger on it," she said.

Axel moved around the car, slipping into the driver's seat. "I'm glad I'm not in his shoes today," he said as his eyes moved up and down Kiera's curves in the figure hugging dress. "I like knowing that I get to peel that dress off of you at the end of the night," he said and took her hands, his thumb rubbing over the beautiful diamond ring he'd put on her finger so recently. "I wouldn't like to figure out how to keep my hands off of you," he said and kissed her gently so he didn't mess up her lipstick.

"Are you ready for some fun?" he asked, looking down at her with pride in his eyes.

She laughed softly. "Now that we get more than a wedding, I'm more than ready. This should be an interesting day," she said and linked her fingers through his.

He suddenly stopped and turned to her, his eyes serious as he said, "I haven't told you that I love you today," he said, his voice warm and husky as he bent to kiss her gently.

She sighed with happiness. "Yes you did," she said. "Not in words, but in all the small, wonderful things you did this morning."

Axel thought about their morning and raised an eyebrow. "Small?" he asked suggestively.

Kiera rolled her eyes, trying not to laugh. "Not all things were small," she clarified, understanding that he was thinking about the way he woke her up this morning with soft, feather-light kisses on her back. All of which turned to not-very-light kisses once she was fully awake. However, she was thinking of the coffee he brought to her in the shower, or the warm towel he wrapped around her after their shower, the delicious eggs he made her with the last of his summer vegetables or the quiet silence as he held her hand while they read the morning paper. "But I love you too," she whispered with all the happiness she was feeling.

Excerpt from "His Secretive Lover"

Ryker smiled inwardly as he pulled into his parking spot, but not a hint of that personal satisfaction showed on his handsome features. Ryker was known to be reserved, cool and in control. He rarely put his emotions on display unless he was alone with his brothers. And even then, he was the eldest, needing to be the calming influence. He knew his responsibilities and took them very seriously.

That didn't mean he couldn't appreciate life, he thought as his eyes looked around for the woman.

To the casual observer, he knew that he generally looked serious and intent but he didn't really care. The opinions of others was of no consequence, he had more important things to worry about than whether someone perceived him as likable. Ryker didn't mind that his staff was intimidated by him. It enabled him to run The Thorpe Group more effectively. He not only had his entire division to run, he was also responsible for the whole company not to mention his three younger brothers who tended to lean towards the boisterous side of life. Thankfully, they didn't fight as much as they used to.

Well, Xander did, but that was because of…Ryker sighed as he thought about that situation. Xander was the second oldest and in charge of the family law division of The Thorpe Group. Ryker thought about the cynicism he'd seen recently in his younger brother. It wasn't healthy and Xander was definitely becoming more jaded. Maybe that's why the arguments between the second oldest and their office manager, Autumn, were getting more…pointed.

Stepping out of his black Tesla sedan, he lifted his briefcase and walked efficiently towards the building's entrance. He timed it perfectly every day and, sure enough, there she was. The exquisite woman with curly blond hair was hurrying into the building on the opposite side of the courtyard. She was lovely and had the sexiest walk, even when she was rushing.

He waited until she was through the doors, watching her for as long as possible before he proceeded into his building. It was a morning ritual that he intended to stop, as soon as he could figure out how to get her to agree to dinner with him. She was painfully shy, he knew. On previous occasions he'd tried to get her attention, but she'd just scurried away after a brief glimpse in his direction.

They played this game every morning, staring at each other across the courtyard, both of them obviously interested but she was too timid and ran away before he could figure out how to interact with her. He'd tried to speak with her once when they ran into each other at the deli. She'd been even more beautiful up close but she'd blushed and hurried out the door, not even getting her lunch in her rush to get away from him. He'd watched her blond curls and extraordinary figure hurry out the door as quickly as her heels could carry her but he'd caught her blush as well as the small gasp that escaped from her lush mouth as soon as she saw him.

A weaker man might be discouraged but not him. That woman was worth the effort, he told himself as he pressed the elevator button for his floor. He would have her sitting across a restaurant table from him very soon. He walked into his office, his assistant, Joan, meeting him at the doorway to the lobby as she did every single morning, following behind him as she read through his early morning messages.

"And lastly, Jason Moran left a message last night and wanted to speak with you urgently. This is his third message in two weeks," she told him without any kind of expression on her face. Joan knew not to be judgmental about any of the issues that came through this office. If her boss hadn't called the man back, there was a reason.

Ryker's eyes slashed over to Joan's. "Jason?" he repeated, his irritation at the man's persistence annoying. "I gave Jason to Martha as a client," he explained, referring to one of the other lawyers in his group. "I know she called him back the last time he called. What does he need to speak with me about?"

Ryker knew that Jason Moran worked in the building across the courtyard. The same building in which his introverted stranger worked. That was a promising development, he thought as he took that message and glanced down at the writing. Perhaps Jason could give him more information about the lovely mystery woman.

Making the decision quickly, he handed the pink square paper back to Joan and continued into his office. "Tell Jason I can see him this afternoon. Give him whatever opening is available on my calendar after my lunch meeting."

Joan nodded and made a note, then turned and walked out of his office to follow his instructions.

Cricket leaned against the back of her office door, breathing deeply of the cool air and trying to slow down her frantic heart rate. She couldn't believe that she felt like this just because that man watched her walk into the building. Even from a distance, the look was so hot, so intense she felt like she was going to burn up as she walked from the parking garage to the door to the building.

Often, on her drive into the office, she tried to talk herself into actually looking at the man. She'd seen him up close once and he was…amazing! She'd been such a wimp that day. She'd seen his intention to talk to her, to actually communicate, but she'd run away. It was one thing to have a secret infatuation with a man, to build up stories about him and wonder what it would be like to actually talk to him and meet him. She imagined herself sitting down with him in a fancy, elegant restaurant, enjoying witty repartee while he laughed at her quick wit and pithy observations.

Alas, she wasn't quick witted and she rarely had profound reflections about people other than whether they had adequate security or if their jewelry was real or fake. Other than that, her life revolved around numbers and finding the stories in the numbers. She might be able to sneak into a high security building without being noticed or find variances down to the penny in a multi-million dollar project, but conversing with a gorgeous man? Nope, she was too shy. Especially around her tall, terrifyingly huge and intimidating morning-man in particular.

She really needed to change her schedule so she wasn't showing up at the exact same moment he was arriving each day. But then she smiled inside her tiny office where no one else could see, her body's reaction slowing down. As long as he continued to arrive at the same time, she'd probably keep the same schedule that had her driving up at the same moment. Her mind relished the zing that she got from his look each morning. The feeling was better than a double shot of espresso. It might be silly, looking forward to seeing a man every morning, but she loved her morning excitement. If she changed her schedule, she'd miss that man terribly.

She should be brave and just talk to the guy. She set her alarm clock, skipped breakfast if she was running late, went around the block a few times if she was early…all so she could get a glimpse of him each morning. It was more than a little pathetic, she told herself.

But the idea of actually talking to him, of meeting him face to face instead of across the courtyard set her whole body to shivering in fear. What would she say to him? What could they possibly have in common? He looked like some sort of executive while she was a lowly accountant. She'd probably trip on her own feet if she got any closer to him. He made her so nervous just with a look!

With a sigh, she sat down behind her desk and pulled her chair in close, turning on her computer and pulling the large stack of messy and poorly written expense reports closer, forcing her mind away from one dazzling, sexy and scary man. Now that she'd had her morning jolt it was time to start her day. She might be a boring, cautious accountant but that didn't mean she wasn't also a secret adrenaline junkie.

COMMENTS FROM THE AUTHOR

For some fun visuals on Axel and Kiera, go to:

http://www.pinterest.com/elennoxromances/his-unexpected-lover-kiera-and-axel/

If you have time, please take a moment to write a review on whichever platform you purchased this book. It not only helps guide others who might purchase this book, but I also love hearing from my readers – the good, the bad and the ugly. Some readers tell me there's too much sex, some tell me I should add more, others criticize my grammar and others tell me they love my books. Everything you write, I use to improve my next story. If you love what I write, let me know because I'll continue writing in the same way. If you think I should improve in some way, please let me know. I have a very tough skin and can take it – although I absolutely LOVE the positive reviews/comments.

If you would like to contact me directly, I can be reached at elizabeth@elizabethlennox.com. I try very hard to answer all e-mails because I love hearing from readers so much! It is a thrill to hear from you. But I apologize in advance if I miss responding to your message. Sometimes, things get lost in the inbox. I'm one of those non-techy people so I don't always see things that others might think are obvious. It isn't a slight – I promise. It is just that my mind is off in romance-world and not in the techy-world (much more fun/interesting/exciting in my romance-world even though my husband bangs his head against the desk sometimes when I don't understand the techy-world).

BOOKS BY ELIZABETH LENNOX

The Texas Tycoon's Temptation

The Royal Cordova Trilogy
Escaping a Royal Wedding
The Man's Outrageous Demands
Mistress To The Prince

The Attracelli Family Series
Never Dare A Tycoon
Falling For The Boss
Risky Negotiations
Proposal To Love
Love's Not Terrifying
Romantic Acquisition

The Billionaire's Terms: Prison Or Passion
The Sheik's Love Child
The Sheik's Unfinished Business
The Greek Tycoon's Lover
The Sheik's Sensuous Trap
The Greek's Baby Bargain
The Italian's Bedroom Deal
The Billionaire's Gamble
The Tycoon's Seduction Plan
The Sheik's Rebellious Mistress
The Sheik's Missing Bride
Blackmailed By The Billionaire
The Billionaire's Runaway Bride
The Billionaire's Elusive Lover
The Intimate, Intricate Rescue
The Sisterhood Trilogy
The Sheik's Virgin Lover
The Billionaire's Impulsive Lover
The Russian's Tender Lover
The Billionaire's Gentle Rescue

The Tycoon's Toddler Surprise

The Tycoon's Tender Triumph
The Sheik's Mysterious Mistress
The Duke's Willful Wife
The Sheik's Secret Twins
The Tycoon's Marriage Exchange
The Russian's Furious Fiancée
The Tycoon's Misunderstood Bride

Love By Accident Series
The Sheik's Pregnant Lover
The Sheik's Furious Bride
The Duke's Runaway Princess

The Russian's Pregnant Mistress

The Lovers Exchange Series
The Earl's Outrageous Lover
The Tycoon's Resistant Lover

The Sheik's Reluctant Lover
The Spanish Tycoon's Temptress

The Berutelli Escape Series
Resisting The Tycoon's Seduction
The Billionaire's Secretive Enchantress

The Big Apple Brotherhood
The Billionaire's Pregnant Lover
The Sheik's Rediscovered Lover
The Tycoon's Defiant Southern Belle

The Sheik's Dangerous Lover (free novella)

The Thorpe Brothers Series
His Captive Lover
His Unexpected Lover
His Secretive Lover
His Challenging Lover

The Sheik's Defiant Fiancée (Free Novella)

The Prince's Resistant Lover (Free Novella)
The Tycoon's Make Believe Fiancée (Free Novella)

The Friendship Series
The Billionaires Masquerade
The Russian's Dangerous Game
The Sheik's Beautiful Intruder

The Love and Danger Series – Romantic Mysteries
Intimate Desires
Intimate Caresses
Intimate Secrets – July 2014
Intimate Whispers – August 2014